The Gunman's Mistake

"Help? You want my help? This I'll give you!"

And Laib Domb reached into a desk drawer and pulled out a revolver.

He is a very stupid man, Weiss thought, removing his hands from his pockets and slowly backing toward the door.

"Don't do anything that you will regret," he said as he reached behind him for the doorknob. Weiss turned the knob and pushed the door open with his back.

Noise came through the open door.

"I'll show you what I do to pests," Laib Domb said.

He aimed the revolver in Weiss's general direction.

Weiss raised his hands over his head.

It took the club owner only an instant to realize that he might have made a mistake. He and the detective were in full view of the large room and its patrons.

Murder in Gotham

ISIDORE HAIBLUM

BERKLEY PRIME CRIME, NEW YORK

THE BERKLEY PUBLISHING GROUP
Published by the Penguin Group
Penguin Group (USA) Inc.
375 Hudson Street, New York, New York 10014, USA
Penguin Group (Canada), 90 Eglinton Avenue East, Suite 700, Toronto, Ontario M4P 2Y3, Canada
(a division of Pearson Penguin Canada Inc.)
Penguin Books Ltd., 80 Strand, London WC2R 0RL, England
Penguin Group Ireland, 25 St. Stephen's Green, Dublin 2, Ireland (a division of Penguin Books Ltd.)
Penguin Group (Australia), 250 Camberwell Road, Camberwell, Victoria 3124, Australia
(a division of Pearson Australia Group Pty. Ltd.)
Penguin Books India Pvt. Ltd., 11 Community Centre, Panchsheel Park, New Delhi—110 017, India
Penguin Group (NZ), 67 Apollo Drive, Rosedale, North Shore 0632, New Zealand
(a division of Pearson New Zealand Ltd.)
Penguin Books (South Africa) (Pty.) Ltd., 24 Sturdee Avenue, Rosebank, Johannesburg 2196,
South Africa

Penguin Books Ltd., Registered Offices: 80 Strand, London WC2R 0RL, England

This is a work of fiction. Names, characters, places, and incidents either are the product of the author's imagination or are used fictitiously, and any resemblance to actual persons, living or dead, business establishments, events, or locales is entirely coincidental. The publisher does not have any control over and does not assume any responsibility for author or third-party websites or their content.

MURDER IN GOTHAM

A Berkley Prime Crime Book / published by arrangement with the author

PRINTING HISTORY
Berkley Prime Crime mass-market edition / January 2008

Copyright © 2008 by Isidore Haiblum.
Cover art by Jeff Crosby.
Cover design by Steven Ferlauto.
Interior text design by Kristin del Rosario.

ISBN: 978-0-425-21907-2

BERKLEY® PRIME CRIME
Berkley Prime Crime Books are published by The Berkley Publishing Group,
a division of Penguin Group (USA) Inc.,
375 Hudson Street, New York, New York 10014.
The name BERKLEY PRIME CRIME and the BERKLEY PRIME CRIME design
are trademarks of Penguin Group (USA) Inc.

PRINTED IN THE UNITED STATES OF AMERICA

10 9 8 7 6 5 4 3 2 1

To my beautiful wife, Ruthie, whose wit, intelligence, and humor were indispensable in the creation of this book. The honeymoon continues. . . .

Acknowledgments

A tip of the hat to Stuart Silver, whom I've known forever and who is always there for me; my thanks to Jerry Marcus, my Yiddish-speaking cohort who helps keep my Yiddish alive and well; and to T. E. D. Klein, my friend and colleague who helped keep the creative juices flowing during the writing of this book; a dozen roses for my peerless agent, Nancy Yost, and my wonderful editor, Michelle Vega. To my wife, Ruth, thanks for keeping me sitting up and walking straight, making sure my characters sang in the right key and my jokes rang true. And, as always, special thanks for their support and encouragement to: John dePillis, Susan Husserl-Kapit, Ellie Faust, Phyllis and Arthur Skoy, Annie Zeybekoglu, Judith A. Yablonky, and her cat, Foxy La Rue.

One

Crime doesn't pay if you are caught and can't afford a good lawyer. Unless, of course, you know a private detective who can get you off scot-free. There are a few still around. But modesty prevents me from naming the very best.

FROM THE CASEBOOKS OF MORRIS WEISS

"Find Lefkowitz," Grosebard said. "We will pay."

"With what?" Shmulevitch demanded. "We will steal from the burial fund?"

"God forbid," Fefer said. "The strike fund has plenty of money."

"So," Shmulevitch said, fixing him with a beady eye, "you will steal then from the strike fund?"

"What steal?" Greenberg said, a touch of outrage in his voice. "When was the last time there was a strike at *The Jewish Daily Forward*? The money sits and does nothing. Our paper was once a socialist paper. We have a tradition of supporting our workers."

They were seated at one end of a long table, Morris Weiss and the five union representatives. It was mid-February and snowing outside. The windows of the sixth-floor conference room were frosted over. The sound of traffic from the streets below was distant and muffled. As though they were in a sealed-off world of their own.

Weiss sighed.

Why was everything so hard with these people? You speak to one of them and everything is hunky-dory. But just try to work out something with more than one and you play with your life.

"I won't take money from the strike fund," Weiss said, "and that's flat."

His father, Weiss knew, would have approved. He always held strike funds to be sacrosanct.

Sitting back comfortably in his chair, the detective waited for further developments. He knew that with this crew there would be some if only he were patient. Being patient was something he knew how to do. It came with the job. Although he wasn't crazy about this particular aspect of the job.

Morris Weiss was not only the best-dressed man in the room, but at twenty-nine, also the youngest. He had on a three-piece, chalk-striped black suit, a white shirt with starched collar, and a green-and-gold paisley tie. Idly, he ran a thumb over his black mustache, and watched the others through half-lidded eyes.

The fifth man, tall, cadaverous, and stooped, now spoke up for the first time. "My printers will pay," he said. "Lefkowitz is a brother in good standing. We will do the right thing by him."

Grosebard turned to Weiss.

"You are in agreement?"

The detective shrugged.

"Why wouldn't I be?"

Grosebard frowned.

"Don't give me riddles. A simple yes or no will do."

Weiss nodded.

"Then let it be a simple yes," he said.

Grosebard glared around defiantly.

"Settled!" he shouted. And slammed his hand down on the table.

Two

It never hurts to have a good friend in high places, one who can rewrite the rules in your favor. Just make sure they don't catch him doing it, or even the rewritten rules won't be able to keep you out of the hoosegow.

FROM THE CASEBOOKS OF MORRIS WEISS

"Mrs. Lefkowitz," Weiss said and smiled.

"Please," she said, smiling back, "call me May." She extended a slim, black-gloved hand, which the detective took.

"My pleasure," Morris Weiss said.

"It is not as though we are strangers, Morris."

"God forbid."

No, he thought, *we have met at least twice at gatherings. Maybe even three times. That would be a bonanza. Although it might be stretching things a bit.*

"Morris," she said, "you know it is always a pleasure to see you."

"The feeling is mutual, May."

She sighed.

"If only the circumstances were happier now," she said.

May Lefkowitz was a few inches shorter than the detective's five foot seven, even in high heels. She had on a stylish black, calf-length, square-shouldered dress and a small black triangular hat with a veil over the eyes.

It is not as expensive as it looks, Weiss thought. *I saw the same outfit in Wanamaker's window.*

They were in the fourth-floor office of Solomon Garfinkel, *The Forward*'s features editor, a slim, dapper man in his early sixties. He rose from behind his desk, went around it, shook the detective's hand, and winked.

"I am turning her over to you," he said. To May he said, "Mrs. Lefkowitz, here you have the best detective on the Lower East Side."

And he left.

That man, Weiss thought, *will do anything to escape his office.*

May said, "He spoke very highly of you, Morris."

"He should. I did a job for him. It turned out very well. Usually," Weiss said, "he is a man of few words. You must have inspired him."

"It is you, Morris, I want to inspire."

"Too late, I am already inspired."

She flashed him a broad smile.

"I know your husband, May. He and I have often played chess together."

"I did not know that."

"It's true. He puts up a good fight."

"You beat him?"

Morris shrugged.

"I beat most of them unless they are masters. And even them I beat sometimes. Come," he said, and steered her to the chair behind the desk that Garfinkel had just vacated, then seated himself by its side.

"Morris," she said lowering her eyes, "I don't know how I can pay you."

"That is not a problem," he said.

She shook her head.

"Jake would not want me to take charity."

Weiss raised an eyebrow.

"What charity?" he said.

"So who is paying you?"

"Jake's union branch," he said.

May let out a long sigh.

"That is what unions are for," Weiss said.

"Thank God," she said. "I knew I could never afford you."

Weiss smiled.

"Don't be so sure," he said. "For friends I have bargain prices."

"Morris, you are an angel."

"But a secular one."

Weiss put his elbows on the desk top, leaned forward, and peered at his client.

"So tell me, May, your husband has done something wrong?"

"God forbid. My Jake is an upstanding man."

"Then why haven't you gone to the police if he's been missing for two weeks?"

"The police? What can they do? They are all Irish. For them the Lower East Side is a foreign country."

The woman is right, he thought.

"Which is not so bad for my business," he said.

And smiled.

"If only I could, Morris, I would give you all the business in the world. You know that."

"All would be too much," he said. "What I need from you is a list of his friends, relatives, even acquaintances."

"I will give you what I can," she said.

"Good," Weiss said. "I will do the rest."

"You will?"

"Of course," Morris Weiss said grinning. "That is why they hire me."

"Thank you, Morris," she said blushing.

The detective shrugged.

"It is all in a day's work," he said.

"I knew I could count on you, Morris."

Which is more than I knew, he thought.

"Do not worry, May," he said. "Everything is going to be all right."

And thought: *Weiss to the rescue again.*

Three

---◦◦◦◦◦---

Making money isn't everything. But for lots of people it will do quite well until something better comes along.

FROM THE CASEBOOKS OF MORRIS WEISS

"Me?" Sam Shlusberg said.

Weiss smiled.

"Who else?" he said.

Morris Weiss was in Shlusberg's Quality Cleaning Store on the corner of Grand and Chrystie streets, where he himself was a steady customer. He felt as if he hadn't left home yet. And for good reason. He had almost as much clothing here as in his own closet.

By the plate glass window, Goldfarb the tailor, peddled furiously on his Singer sewing machine. Weiss half expected it to levitate. In the corner, next to the framed blue FDR photograph, sat Stanley the presser, with a hot iron and bottle of water working furiously on a pile of clothing.

If they work this hard, Weiss thought, *why are they*

taking so long with my things? A few weeks more and my clothes will be out of style.

"Jake's wife tells me," he said, "you are a close friend."

Sam Shlusberg shrugged, as though it were news to him.

"See behind me on the rack," he said, "the green jacket is his. Also pants of his I have. That's how well we know each other. Period."

"So you are not a close friend?"

Shlusberg sighed.

"We travel sometimes in the same circles," he said. "That's all."

"Good enough," Weiss said.

And thought: *Why is it so hard to get a straight answer from this man?*

Shlusberg lit an Old Gold, inhaled deeply, and peered at the detective.

"What is good about it?" he said.

"Maybe," Weiss said, "you will be able to tell me what has happened to him?"

"He is really gone?"

"Absolutely."

"That explains why he hasn't picked up his clothes."

"I am glad I could solve this little mystery for you, Shlusberg. Now maybe you can help me with one of mine."

The cleaner nodded.

"I have heard stories," he said.

"Even stories might help," Weiss said.

"Well, for one thing, I have heard that Jake, he is a big gambler."

"No one mentioned that to me," Weiss said.

Not even the wife, he thought. *Maybe she hadn't heard.*

"Twice I have seen it with my own eyes."

"Where?"

"On top of a small candy store."

"Laib Domb the bookie?"

"You know him?"

Weiss smiled.

"What kind of detective would I be," he said, "if I didn't?"

"You are right. So I will tell you more. I have heard that he is up to his neck in debt."

"And you learned this how?"

"From Jake himself."

"He told only you, eh?"

"It is no secret. Everyone knows."

"Who is everyone?"

"His friends."

"Shlusberg, I am one of his friends."

"Yes, but the wrong kind."

"What kind is that?"

"Don't take offense. With you, he plays chess. With them he plays cards and horses. Also he rolls the dice."

So do I, Weiss thought. *But what business is it of his?*

The detective removed a small notebook from his coat pocket.

"Please, Shlusberg," he said. "Give me their names. It is time I became one of his friends, too."

Four

*In the old days, if you got into trouble on the Lower East
Side all you had to do was yell for help in Yiddish and people would come pouring out of their stores to help you.
Today, to play it safe, you had better know a bit of Chi-
nese and Vietnamese, too.*

FROM THE CASEBOOKS OF MORRIS WEISS

Weiss and Ida kissed long and passionately.

Then, to the accompaniment of squeaking bedsprings, they disentangled.

"Those springs made more noise than we did,"
Weiss said in Yiddish. "And we made plenty."

"You should fix them, darling" Ida said, also in
Yiddish.

"I should do a lot of things," he pointed out.

"You always do more than enough."

"I do?"

"Much more."

That is good to know, he thought.

"Thank you. Usually the bedsprings behave themselves perfectly," Weiss said. "They are models of

their kind. Of course, when you are not here, Idaleh, I do not jump up and down on them."

"When am I here? Once in a blue moon."

Weiss smiled. "That is probably why I have never bothered to fix them."

She moved closer and they kissed again.

"Moisheleh," she said.

"Yes, darling."

"I have an idea."

"I will treasure it always," he said.

"I could bring an oilcan next time I come," she said.

"I would treasure that always, too," he said.

"Or," she said, wrapping her legs around him, "we could live together as one in my apartment."

"It is a wonderful apartment," he said. "But so far away."

"Stop it," she said. "The Lower East Side can get along without its great detective."

"All my business is here," he said.

She sighed. "Always the same answer. Is it at least going well?"

"If you mean am I a millionaire?" he said. "Not yet."

Ida curled up against Weiss's shoulder, one leg over his knees, her long glistening black hair spread out on the pillow. They had been lovers for more than three years now. Ida, a violist, was a founding member of the Prometheus string quartet, and often played in pickup orchestras, as well, to make ends meet.

Between his private detective work and her concert appearances, scheduling time together was becoming a problem.

Tonight the pair had gone to hear Arthur Schnabel and Joseph Szigeti at Hunter College in a program of Mozart and Beethoven sonatas. Both proclaimed it an overwhelming experience. They had a late dinner at Moscowits and Lupowitz, a favorite Romanian-Jewish restaurant on East Third Street and Second Avenue, and that had been proclaimed an overwhelming experience, too. They had then retired to the detective's Grand Street fifth-floor walk-up, which was close by, and began making love. This they didn't have to proclaim as an overwhelming experience. It simply was.

"So," Ida said, "when will you be a millionaire?"

"When I stop working for the *Forverts* and start working for Rockefeller."

"So what's keeping you?"

"They haven't asked me yet," Weiss said. "But I am patient."

"Moisheleh, I will be a grandmother by then."

"And still a beauty."

"Thank you, Moisheleh. But until then?"

"You mean now? Absolutely nothing for the next twelve hours."

Ida wrinkled her nose.

"We won't even make love?" she asked.

"We will make love," he said. "We will eat breakfast later. Here."

"You make breakfast, too?"

"You know I do. On Grand Street I am famous for my omelets."

"I've fallen into the right hands," she said.

"You're telling me," he said. "What I meant was that I would not even think of the case, Idaleh. The case will have to take care of itself. And I will take care of you."

"That is very nice of you," she said.

"My pleasure."

"I should hope so, darling," she said, putting a pillow over his face and straddling him.

I will go see the candy store man, Weiss thought, before giving himself over fully to the pleasures of Ida. *He used to know everyone.*

Maybe he still does.

Five

If crime doesn't pay, why are there so many rich lawyers? And why aren't they smart enough to hire more private detectives?

FROM THE CASEBOOKS OF MORRIS WEISS

Weiss opened the door and stepped inside. He saw boxes of chocolate-covered cherries, one-inch wax bottles with sweetened colored water, sugar dots stuck on a narrow roll of paper. *Nothing has changed,* he thought, *but the old man is older.* Of course now there were no newspapers or magazines and only a few comic books as in other candy stores. But then this was no ordinary candy store.

He said, "Good morning, Kressky."

A thin, white-haired man sat behind the counter, a cigarette dangling between narrow lips.

He looked surprised. Then he smiled.

Weiss said, "You remember me, eh?"

"Morry Weiss. From the old store, when you were just a boy." Kressky held out a pack of Pall Malls. *No doubt*, Weiss thought, *to acknowledge that I have finally become a man.*

The detective waved it away.

"I tried once for a day," he said. "I couldn't taste the food I was eating. And when I went walking in the park I smelled nothing."

Kressky sighed. "You are right," he said. "It is a filthy habit, but I am too old to stop."

The detective nodded. *You are never too old to give up a really bad habit*, he thought of saying. But he didn't bother. It wasn't his problem. And Kressky wouldn't listen to him anyway.

Morris Weiss had on a long, wide-shouldered gray tweed overcoat, a blue woolen muffler, and a gray fedora. He also wore galoshes over his black oxfords. Ida had insisted, although the streets were almost clear of snow by now. *That woman takes care of me to a fault*, he thought. *Not that I mind.*

"The week DiMaggio left the army," Kressky said in Yiddish, "I saw you on the street. That was the last time."

"Then you must lead a very sheltered life," Weiss said. "I am always around."

Kressky shrugged.

"Maybe I just didn't notice," he said. "I can get you something? An egg cream?"

The detective settled himself on a stool.

"A cup of coffee," he said. "Black."

Just seeing all those candies has already turned

my stomach, he thought. *And to think as a child I couldn't live without them.*

Kressky reached over and poured Weiss a cup of coffee.

"I have come to see your landlord," the detective said in Yiddish. For that added touch of intimacy. It often brought results. Besides, Weiss enjoyed Yiddish.

"Landlord? Which one?" Kressky said. "We are blessed with two, you know."

Weiss took a swallow of coffee.

"I didn't know," he said.

"Laib Domb and Yankel Gold."

"The first one I know," Weiss said. "Who is this second one?"

"The hidden partner."

"Ah-ha," Weiss said.

"A man like that," Kressky said, "it is better to keep him hidden."

Kressky laughed. And quickly looked around to make sure no one else had heard.

It was a safe bet, Weiss thought. Except for a kid reading a copy of *Action Comics*, the store was empty of customers.

"Very nice place."

Kressky smiled as though he'd been paid a compliment.

"It hasn't changed much over the years," he said.

"You are the lookout?"

"Why not? Why shouldn't it be me?"

"I can give you plenty of reasons."

"Do not bother," Kressky said. "I have heard them all. My relations never stop *hocking* me."

"But you don't listen, eh?"

"Morry, I know you were a Golden Gloves champion, a sergeant in the army, and you are now a detective. Three good jobs and you are still almost a kid. So why shouldn't I make a dollar?"

"Only the last job of mine makes a dollar, Kressky, and sometimes only half a dollar. But it's an honest dollar."

Kressky lit another Pall Mall, took a long drag, and coughed.

Soon, Weiss thought, *he will smoke himself right into a hospital bed, if not someplace worse.*

The outer door swung open and a boy of fifteen or so in knickers and a peaked cap dashed in, nodded to Kressky, and ran through the store for the back room.

"One of the runners," Kressky said. "It is a good job for the boys. They go to our bettors on foot and give them the odds and take their bets and money."

"Very lively. And only a step away from a jail cell."

"The mothers know what goes on upstairs," Kressky said. "They tell the children to buy at Litvinof's two blocks over. Thank God. I did not come here to sell candies. What I do is sit, smoke, listen to the Yiddish radio, read a nice Yiddish paper, maybe. If a stranger comes in here and God forbid looks like he's going to make trouble, I press a button right under the counter and he is soon taken care of. Only the runners come into the store to deliver bets or winnings. They are all boys, so what better place to come to than a candy store? Who pays attention? Besides, the police are taken care of. Morry, a man my age can't stand on his feet all day. Even dealing with children is not such a great pleasure. Now the business upstairs takes care of me."

"I need to see one of the bosses, Kressky."

"Well, these days there is really only one. Laib Domb."

"What happened to the other?"

Kressky shrugged.

"What didn't," he said.

"Meaning what?" Weiss said.

"Who knows?"

Too bad vaudeville is dead, or this man and I could have gone onstage and killed it. We would be famous.

Weiss gave Kressky a hard look.

"If," he said, "you do not tell me this very minute, I will stop buying my candies here."

Kressky smiled at the joke.

"You drive a hard bargain," he said. "What do the kids say these days? Ah, yes, 'the clink.' "

"The clink?"

Kressky nodded happily.

"What kids?" Weiss said. "Hoodlums. Now where is this other partner?"

"He is in the clink—in prison. So Laib Domb is the only one you can see now."

"And where do I find him. Upstairs?"

"He will not see you upstairs. It is where they keep the money. And where those who win or lose big money play. No one goes up there without permission."

"So what is your advice?"

"Listen. On Rivington Street over Fishman's Bakery there is an after-hours club. Laib Domb has an office there, too."

"Why?"

"Why not? He is part owner. I will give you the password."

"Thank you."

"Do not mention it. And do not gamble there. It is all fixed, you know."

"I know," Weiss said.

Six

◆

It is an excellent thing to have a wife who is a classical musician. If nothing else, listening to her play great music will help take your mind off how dishonest people can be.

FROM THE CASEBOOKS OF MORRIS WEISS

First of all, Morris Weiss thought, *it was nothing like the movies. And nothing like the fancy uptown clubs, where I sometimes drop by. Here half the crowd speaks Yiddish, the other half broken English. And they are almost all men. Where are the beautiful young women in low-cut gowns? The club walls here do not glitter with mirrors and lights.* White paint peeled off in spots revealing the ancient blue paint underneath. Through thick cigarette and cigar smoke, Weiss recognized some faces from the neighborhood. Mostly poor workers and shopkeepers; they couldn't afford to lose. But lose they would. *Well, no one is forcing them to come here.* From Fishman's Bakery below Weiss could smell fresh bread baking. *At least something's wholesome*, he thought.

The detective moved slowly through the crowd, stopping to watch some of the games. He was surprised to see how many people he knew. Some had even been clients in the past.

He chose those first.

Yankel Glants appeared amazed to see him.

"What are you doing here, Weiss? I thought you were a sensible fellow. I didn't know you were a fellow addict."

"I'm not," Weiss said.

"Is business so bad," Glants said, "that you must come to this place to make a few extra cents?"

Weiss smiled. "Business will never be this bad."

"Ah, then the criminals are not yet behaving themselves?"

"They still act like criminals," Weiss said.

Glants grinned.

"Thank God, I could not stand it if everything changed overnight."

"Glants, you are absolutely safe," Weiss said.

Glants was a *Forverts* writer. He rewrote news stories from the English language wire services and every Friday wrote a humor column.

"So, what are you doing here, Weiss, slumming?"

"Looking for our mutual friend."

"Lefkowitz, eh?"

The detective nodded.

"The whole Lower East Side is *tumeling* about this disappearance."

"Good."

"I think so, too. Anything that will help find Jake, I'm for."

"You have the right attitude," Weiss said.

"Of course. I should have the wrong one?"

"Then do me a favor."

"You have only to name it."

"While you are here," Weiss said, "spread the word that I am looking for Jake."

"It will be my pleasure. Do you want me to hand out circulars, too?"

"Don't trouble yourself."

The writer turned to go.

"By the way," Weiss said, "how is your son?"

The writer's son, Marvin, had run away from home last year. Weiss had found him.

"He does well, thank you."

"You should spend more time with him," Weiss said. And even as he said it, thinking it was not the smartest advice he had ever given.

"I will bear that in mind."

The two men shook hands and Glants vanished into the crowd.

Imagine, Glants is a regular here, Weiss thought, *and I didn't even know it. I should hire a detective myself to keep track of these things.*

During the next hour and a half Weiss repeated a variation of his conversation with Glants with a few dozen others. No one knew where Jake Lefkowitz was, but they all offered to help find him.

Jake is more popular now, Weiss thought, *than he ever was working a printing press. If he ever starts winning instead of losing here, he could even run for office.*

Provided, of course, he is still alive.

Weiss retrieved his coat from the hatcheck girl, gave her a big fifty-cent tip, left, and went down a long flight of stairs.

Who knows, he thought, *maybe something will come of this yet.*

But remembering where he was, he decided not to bet on it. *Any bet I make here, even with myself, is bound to lose. The place is so crooked the air feels jinxed.*

A middle-aged man in a gray suit stepped over to the detective.

"I would like a word with you sir."

"About what?"

"A possible job."

"So tell me about it," Weiss said.

"Not here. Let us step into the washroom."

"After you."

The two men made their way through the crowd, down a side corridor, and into a dank washroom. Weiss's companion held his index finger up to his lips, stepped over to a urinal, and flushed it. He also flushed both toilets and turned on the water in both sinks.

Then the man turned to Weiss.

"My name is Irving Blottnick. I represent a group of fellow gamblers who come here regularly. We have been losing more than usual. We believe this place is even more crooked than before, and it was plenty crooked then. But you could still win and sometimes win big. My friends and I would like to hire you, Mr. Weiss, to find out what is going on and if necessary to expose this bunch. Understand, Mr. Weiss, this gambling is serious recreation for us. So what do you say?"

This man Blottnick and his friends must be the last gamblers in the city to have learned that this place is completely fixed. Still, their money, as far as I'm concerned, is a good as anyone's.

"Even if you can get rid of current management, the people who take their place will, sooner or later, start doing the same tricks."

"All this will take time, and meanwhile with new people in place we stand a chance of playing an honest game," Blottnick said.

"Okay, Blottnick, I accept."

Weiss reached into his pocket and handed the man a business card.

"Come and see me during office hours. Call first so your trip is not wasted."

"Now," Blottnick said. "How much do you charge?"

"Much less than you are losing here," the detective said.

Seven

❦

Watch out! Having interrogated suspects yourself will be no help at all should you, God forbid, become a suspect. Get a good lawyer fast.

FROM THE CASEBOOKS OF MORRIS WEISS

Two stocky men were waiting outside the club in the dark.

"You Weiss?"

"The same," Weiss said.

"We're all gonna take a friendly little walk together."

"How nice," Weiss said, moving a half step back, and turning his left shoulder slightly, the better to deliver or block a punch, if necessary. He was not especially concerned. These two would be no problem.

"The boss wants to see you."

"Ah-ha. And he is?"

"Laib Domb."

"You don't say?" Weiss said, a smile on his face. "One of my favorite people," he said. And thought,

Maybe this is going to be a good night's work, after all. You can never tell.

"Quick, back inside. The boss don't like to be kept waiting."

"Who does?" Weiss said pleasantly enough.

Weiss turned as a heavy hand pushed him forward.

The detective hated to be pushed. But there was pushing and pushing. He was being led to Laib Domb. *These boys*, he thought, *deserve a tip, not a broken jaw.*

Weiss entered through the club's back door.

The trio went up the stairs, the two men close behind the detective, as if afraid he might suddenly bound up the steps and keep going right through the ceiling.

If these two were any closer, he thought, *they'd be in my hip pocket.*

He was back in the smoke-filled room. *I hate this place*, he thought. *But business is business. And this is in a good cause. I hope.* Once again he squared his shoulders as he stepped inside the room.

A pair of what had to be bouncers loitered near the door as he went in.

They hardly glanced at Weiss, but glance they did.

These two might give me trouble. They are professionals, not hoodlums. Not like the pair on either side of me who behave like prison guards taking a convict to the warden's office.

He was beginning to dislike his two guards intensely.

They came to an unmarked door. No windows here, but by the smell, Weiss knew they were right over Fishman's Bakery.

"In there," one of the men said.

Weiss looked at the door, then glanced back at the crowd. To his surprise at least a dozen faces were gazing back at him. He knew who they were, too. Casual friends from his neighborhood, a runaway husband he had tracked down, two ex-clients. Most of the others just stared at him. A few shook their heads. One small man ran his index finger across his throat.

Well, management doesn't have many friends here, Weiss thought. *But I do.*

The detective nodded to the onlookers.

Six hands waved at him. Then fifteen. Then twenty.

"Make it snappy," one of the hoodlums growled at him.

"Of course," Morris Weiss said. And thought, *Him I won't forget.*

He opened the door.

Eight

Catching lowlifes can best be done by the police. This is a secret I try to keep from my clients.

FROM THE CASEBOOKS OF MORRIS WEISS

"So you're Weiss, eh?"

"And you are the famous Laib Domb."

"I've heard about you."

"Nice things I hope?"

"Yeah. You're a troublemaker, a meddler, and a damn snoop. You've got a wise mouth, too."

"All in a day's work," Weiss said cheerfully.

"Not in my club."

"My friend, this has nothing to do with you or your club."

Laib Domb rose behind his desk. He was a short, corpulent man in his midforties with a red face and long strands of black hair that he combed carefully over his bald dome.

He pointed a finger at Weiss.

"Out!" he shouted.

The detective ignored him. Hands in coat pockets, he gazed serenely at the short, fat man behind the large desk.

"Mr. Domb," he said. "One of your regulars, Jake Lefkowitz, has disappeared. His wife and friends, as you might imagine, are very worried. Any help you could give me would be greatly appreciated."

"Help? You want my help? This I'll give you!"

And Laib Domb reached into a desk drawer and pulled out a revolver.

He is a very stupid man, Weiss thought, removing his hands from his pockets and slowly backing toward the door.

"Don't do anything that you will regret," he said as he reached behind him for the doorknob. Weiss turned the knob and pushed the door open with his back.

Noise came through the open door.

"I'll show you what I do to pests," Laib Domb said.

He aimed the revolver in Weiss's general direction.

Weiss raised his hands over his head.

It took the club owner only an instant to realize that he might have made a mistake. He and the detective were in full view of the large room and its patrons.

"Hey!" he yelled. "What the hell're you doing?"

"Being submissive," the detective said sweetly.

The din behind him instantly changed to dead silence and then began to rise as he knew it would.

"I didn't tell you to do *that*," Laib Domb sputtered.

Weiss's two escorts suddenly appeared on either side of him and tried to pin his arms. Weiss hoped he would have time to take a swing at one of them. But he didn't. Almost immediately he was set free as the crowd surged forward into the office.

"Hey! This is private business," Laib Domb yelled. "Get out!"

The crowd made a beeline for the club owner.

"Good luck," Weiss said, "you'll need it."

And left the office grinning.

Nine

If everyone spoke Yiddish, the language would hardly be as special as it is today. But it would certainly be easier to get around town speaking it.

FROM THE CASEBOOKS OF MORRIS WEISS

Weiss stood downstairs in front of Fishman's Bakery, hands thrust in pockets, and looked through the plate glass window. He saw a half dozen figures wearing long white aprons carrying trays full of freshly baked challah, rye bread, cookies, pies, and cakes.

It's only two thirty in the morning, and already my appetite is getting the better of me. I owe it to Laib Domb, of course. If not for him I'd be sound asleep right now. Still, there are worse things that could be happening.

From up above he heard a commotion coming from the gambling club: the patrons taking on the strong-arm boys. *On my behalf, no less. Maybe my new popularity has already spread to the bakery?*

And I'll be deluged with free samples from their ovens. Why not? I'll try it.

The detective knocked on the bakery window.

After a while someone noticed. A woman in a flour-sprinkled baker's apron impatiently motioned him away.

Undaunted, he stepped over to the door and knocked again.

I am persistent if I am anything, he thought, smiling at himself. *Especially in pursuit of a slice of pie at two in the morning. Or even a cookie.*

One of the bakers finally opened the door, stuck his head out, and said, "Can't you see? We are closed. Come back in the morning. We open at six."

Morris Weiss gave him his name.

"The detective?"

"The very same."

"It is a great pleasure to meet you, Mr. Weiss."

"The pleasure is all mine," Weiss said.

Having a baker on your side, Weiss thought, *is not such a bad thing. I already have some bakers, the bunch from Odessa. But you can never have too many.*

The detective was asked to enter and was given a tour of the bakery along with a very large slice of apple pie and everyone's best wishes.

He left in a very good mood.

I really didn't know my standing in the community was this high, he thought, back on Rivington Street. *Especially among bakers.*

"Mr. Weiss?"

It was a young man in a black leather jacket, with blond hair and mustache. He wore round, wire-rimmed glasses and a peaked checkered cap.

"What can I do for you?" Weiss said.

"I was in the club just now."

"Really? How is everything up there?"

"Bedlam."

The detective smiled.

"What a shame," he said. "They should learn to take better care of their property."

"Mr. Weiss, I heard you are looking for Jake Lefkowitz."

"That is true. You know him?"

"No. My friend Bernie Loft knows him."

"That sounds hopeful."

"Not exactly. Lefkowitz owes him money, and he hasn't paid it back yet."

"So you are saying they are no longer friends?"

"I wouldn't know."

"Why not?"

"Because it looks like Bernie has disappeared, too."

Ten

If you have solved many cases, the mere mention of your name will put fear in the hearts of lowlifes. Better yet, and much safer, would be if they didn't even know your name.

FROM THE CASEBOOKS OF MORRIS WEISS

It's an epidemic of missing men, *Weiss thought,* sticking his gloved hands back in his pockets and looking around. The neighborhood was mostly closed down for the night.

"Come with me," he said.

The detective led the young man back to Fishman's Bakery. Overhead, the war was still going on. Weiss knocked on the glass door, while glancing up to make sure some heavy object didn't come flying out and land on his head. The door opened. This time he was greeted as an old friend.

"So what is it, Mr. Weiss?" the stout woman clad in a white baker's outfit asked in Yiddish. She was smiling broadly, her hands planted on her hips. "Another nice slice of pie, maybe?"

"Thank you very much," Weiss said, also in Yiddish. "But right now only a quiet corner so I can have a few words with this young man."

"This is detective business?"

"What else?"

"Follow me, then."

Weiss and the young man were presently seated at a small yellow table not too far away from the ovens. The aroma was wonderful. But the corner was hot.

Weiss unbuttoned his overcoat, folded it carefully on one of the empty chairs, but kept his gray fedora on his head.

"First," the detective said, "who are you?"

"I am Yossel Korn. My mother calls me Yosseleh, my friends call me Yossie. I live near here on Third Street."

"I will call you Yossie, then. What do you do for a living, Yossie?"

"I am a carpenter."

"Ah," Weiss said. "Good honest work. And your friend Bernie?"

"He works for the radio station WEVD."

"Ah-ha," Weiss said. "Well, that could be honest work, too, if you disregarded the commercials."

The detective had once been on a case for the station. He hesitated to say anything really damning about their programming now.

Along with most Yiddish-speaking Jews living in New York, Weiss knew the station quite well, and sometimes even listened to it. Except when they were playing the Barry Sisters, whom he could not stand.

WEVD incorporated the initials of socialist leader and several-time presidential candidate, Eugene Victor Debs, and were the call letters of New York's Yiddish-language radio station.

"And he does what there?"

"He is their transcription department."

"All by himself?"

"Sure. After all, it's not CBS."

Weiss nodded.

That was for sure.

The detective said, "He has been missing how long?"

"A whole week."

"You reported this to the police?"

"First thing."

"And?"

Yossie shrugged.

"Of course," Weiss said. "It is not a high priority for them. Bernie is over twenty-one?"

Yossie nodded. "His last birthday."

"So much for that. If you are not a criminal or mixed up with them you are responsible for yourself. So, is Bernie a criminal?"

"God forbid."

Weiss asked, "What would you like me to do?"

"If you run across him, could you maybe let me know, Mr. Weiss? His mother is worried."

"And his father isn't?"

"His father is, too."

"So everyone's worried, eh, Yossie?"

"Everyone."

"I will let you know," Weiss said. "You have my word. Especially if you give me your address and phone number."

"Here." The young man gave it to him.

"Thank you."

The two men rose.

"Mr. Weiss, you think it's too early to buy something to eat here?"

"It is never too early if you have the right connections," Weiss said with a straight face. "Come with me."

Eleven

The lowlifes have little job security. This is mostly because of their stupidity and the fact that people like myself are on the job.

FROM THE CASEBOOKS OF MORRIS WEISS

"They cut this Gold loose," Sergeant O'Toole said.

"When?" Weiss said.

"It's been almost a full month now. But fortunately, he's back behind bars again."

O'Toole was a large, heavyset man with a ruddy complexion, small blue eyes, and dark hair, cut very short.

He waved his visitor to a chair.

Weiss shrugged out of his overcoat, put it carefully over the back of the wooden folding chair, and seated himself next to O'Toole's desk.

The station house was surprisingly quiet for eleven in the morning. He could smell Lysol, and could hear the occasional ringing of a phone.

"Why was he let go in the first place?" Weiss asked.

"The victim recanted."

"He did what?"

"Swore it was all a mistake."

Weiss allowed himself a smile.

"The poor man," O'Toole said, "was beaten within an inch of his life. But after recanting, he changed his mind again. We have hidden him away now for his own good."

"So, Sergeant O'Toole, what was it all about?"

"Money, Mr. Weiss, what else?"

"A bad loan, eh?"

"A gambling debt it was."

"And they sent this Gold the Butcher to collect?"

O'Toole laughed.

"He sent himself," he said.

"He is a bookie?"

"That he was before he landed in the hoosegow."

"And," Weiss said, "he is called 'the Butcher' because—?"

"His father was a kosher butcher on Essex Street. But that's only the half of it. See, no matter how hard up a man might be, Gold would extract what was owed him no matter what. And ten percent on top of that to pay for the extra trouble. That is why he was given his honorific, 'the Butcher.'"

"A financial term, eh?"

"And one of respect," O'Toole said.

Both men smiled.

They were old friends. From prewar days when O'Toole walked a beat on Broome Street and Weiss was just beginning to box in the amateurs. O'Toole was a regular at the local clubs. A friend of James J. Braddock, the "Cinderella Man" who beat Max Baer for the heavyweight championship in an upset decision. And he knew Jimmy McLarnin, the ex-welterweight champ. Now, O'Toole was vice president of the Sergeant's Benevolent Association/Superior Officers Council PDNY, and a good man to know—especially for a private detective on the Lower East Side. Despite their long relationship, the two men still addressed each other formally.

"So," Weiss said, "do I visit this Gold in his cell?"

O'Toole grinned.

"Would you settle for the wife?"

"The wife? Of course, that would be excellent."

"Her we know where to find. The son's had his share of run-ins with the law and she stood bail for him on more than one occasion in the past. And being one of your people, you're bound to do better than our lads."

"I usually do better than your lads anyway," Morris Weiss said.

"Especially with elderly women," O'Toole said.

Both men laughed uproariously.

Before leaving, the detective gave his friend the names of the people he'd heard of yesterday.

"You've been a busy man, Mr. Weiss."

The detective sighed.

"Too busy," he said. "With too little results."

Twelve

Some things are not what they seem. Which is a good thing for people like myself, or there would be no work for any of us.

FROM THE CASEBOOKS OF MORRIS WEISS

Weiss knocked on the door.

"Please, in a second," a woman's voice said in Yiddish.

"Do not rush yourself," Weiss said in Yiddish. "I have enough time."

From down the street, he could hear the shoppers on Hester Street, which was packed with overflowing pushcarts and stands and tables full of fruits and vegetables. A crush of shoppers jammed the block. Small stores selling cheap clothing, sour pickles from the barrel, shoes, linens, and hardware items lined both sides of the street.

Just getting through that crowd takes nerves of steel, he thought.

The door finally opened.

"Yes?"

Weiss saw a gray-haired, carefully dressed woman of medium height in a light blue pleated skirt and pink blouse. Her shoes were black and sensibly low heeled.

The living room behind her was neat, clean, and warm. A silver radiator, under a brightly curtained window, hissed steam into the room. A thick carpet covered the floor. A vase filled with artificial flowers sat on a small table which was placed in the exact center under the still life that decorated her wall. *The Daily Mirror*, one of the city's three tabloids—if you didn't count the communist *Daily Worker*—was on the sofa.

"You are Fraydela Gold?" the detective asked.

She gave him a yes.

"My name," he said, "is Morris Weiss, and I am looking for your son."

"Please," she said, "come in. Which son are you looking for, Mr. Weiss?"

"You have more than one?"

"Who doesn't? Albert. Leo. And Joey. No evil eye should befall them. Please, give me your coat. Can I bring you a glass of tea?"

Weiss gave her his coat and hat, both of which went into the hall closet.

"Tea would be nice," he said. "Thank you."

"Come," she said.

Weiss followed her into the kitchen, seated himself

at a small, square wooden table. Soon, he and his hostess were each drinking a glass of tea with lemon and sugar cubes and chatting away in Yiddish as though they were old friends.

"I am looking for, if you will pardon me, the one they call the Butcher."

"I have heard him called worse," she said. "That would be either Joey, my youngest, or my husband. They are both called the Butcher. Joey is sometimes my husband's lieutenant. What have they done now?"

"Nothing that I know of."

"That is good. You are a policeman?"

Weiss shook his head.

"Are we talking about my boy?"

Weiss said yes. "I just need some information."

"That is what they all say."

Weiss put down his tea glass.

"You have had some experience doing this, I see," he said.

"More than a mother needs."

"Well, Mrs. Gold, I promise you, this will be short and absolutely painless. Take my word for it."

She sighed.

"Of course. Right away I saw you were a fine, *hamish* gentleman," she said. "And for a young man, you speak such a fine Yiddish."

"Thank you," the detective said. "Even for an old man," he couldn't resist adding.

"My boys, despite my best efforts, will not speak our language."

"That is too bad," Weiss said with genuine feeling.

"Would you like an egg cookie?" she asked.

Weiss smiled broadly.

"My dear Mrs. Gold, I have never been known to turn down an egg cookie."

If I had a violin, he thought, *and knew how to play it, I could serenade her. Maybe my love of her egg cookies will be good enough.*

Mrs. Gold rose, hurried to a shelf near the oven, and returned with a cloth-covered plate of cookies. He took one, all but smacked his lips, and reached for another.

A performance worthy of a Paul Muni, he thought. *But the cookies are very good.*

"Delicious," he said. *At least I'm not lying*, he thought. *That counts for something. Someday maybe I'll figure out for what.*

He said, "I need to speak with your son about a Jake Lefkowitz . . ."

Mrs. Gold threw back her head and laughed.

"That's what this is about, Jake?"

"What else?"

"I can tell you anything you want to know."

"Your husband, the Butcher, confides in you, eh?" *About his victims*, Weiss was going to add, but thought better of it. He was beginning to regret "the Butcher" part, too.

"No," Mrs. Gold said. "He tells me nothing."

"Nothing?"

"Jake does. We are good friends."

"You know where he is?"

"In hiding."

"He owes money?"

"That, too."

The detective helped himself to another cookie.

"So what is the problem?" he asked.

"He ran off with my son's girlfriend."

Weiss raised an eyebrow. Here was a whole side of Lefkowitz he knew nothing about. Obviously, the man liked to live dangerously.

"Which son?" he said.

"Which son," Mrs. Gold said, "do you think?"

"That one, eh? That's not so good."

"The girl is called Sally Longrin, a blond *shiksa*. What, Mr. Weiss, is the world coming to?"

Weiss smiled.

"The world, alas, does not confide in me," he said.

Mrs. Gold sighed.

"I can understand what Joey was doing with her," she said. "That's not hard. He was doing what he always does."

Weiss shrugged.

"But Jake?" she said.

"He should have known better, eh?"

"Jake is a decent man. And married to a wonderful woman. What could he possibly see in this Sally person?"

"It is a mystery. Maybe if you tell me where I can find her I will solve this mystery, along with what happened to Jake."

"Wait, I will go find the address."

She didn't take long. Only long enough for Weiss to help himself to another cookie.

The detective looked at the piece of paper she handed him. And made a face.

"This Sally, she lives in Sea Gate?"

"No."

"Then what is she doing there?"

"Hiding."

"With Jake?"

"Of course."

Naturally. What could be simpler?

"Hiding from your son, eh?"

"Who else?"

"Maybe the people to whom he owes money?"

"I'm sure you are right, Mr. Weiss."

"I am usually right about such things," he said smiling sweetly. "It is one of my specialties."

Thirteen

A private detective gets to travel to interesting places, many of which he fervently hopes never to see again.

FROM THE CASEBOOKS OF MORRIS WEISS

Sea Gate was at the very tip of Coney Island. Morris Weiss hadn't been there for a good two years. And that time he'd been on a case, too. Before then he had come here with his mother as an eight-year-old. One incident still stuck in his mind. An ancient Model T Ford, of which there were still many in those days, had gone out of control—horn blaring, lights blinking, wheels racing around a grassy oval—and his mother had dashed with him for the protection of a ramshackle, unpainted wooden porch. She was dead certain that the car had gone insane and would head directly for them. Only her timely intervention, she felt, had saved them from a terrible injury, if not even worse. His mother, alas, knew nothing about machines. But she was a very good cook. Weiss had no doubt that these two traits balanced each other out perfectly.

And here he was, back again. Of all places.

This had once been an exclusive enclave for the rich and very rich. All gone now, of course. Even he could afford a cottage in this neighborhood. But who would want to live here now? Who would even want to visit? Weiss continued to drive, his mood taking an uncharacteristic nosedive.

This will lead to nothing, he thought gloomily. *But business is business. And for business you keep on going. And even take some chances. Wasting your time is one of them.*

At least he knew his way around from the days his parents summered at Sea Gate. That should help.

Soon Weiss came to a well-remembered intersection. *Ah-ha*, he thought. And without any hesitation turned left.

He rode through a white world: white lawns, white houses, white trees. There were no tire tracks on the ground at all. He hoped the whole district hadn't been scared off by the inclement weather, making this trip even more worthless than it now seemed.

He saw the house number while passing. He twisted the wheel, skidded, and managed to drive back.

Morris Weiss climbed out of the car, stood in two inches of snow, and gazed at the two-story wood-and-shingle home. Snow covered, it was hardly an imposing sight.

Isidore Haiblum

All the windows were dark.

Maybe Jake and this Sally have gone to bed already. Or maybe they left. Or more likely have never been here at all.

Maybe all this is about Lefkowitz cheating on his wife.

The union delegates would be in for a shock. They would hate it. I wouldn't like it very much myself, he thought.

Weiss took a jimmy from the trunk of his car.

He walked up to the front door. No one answered his knock. He walked around to the back. That door was locked, too. Weiss used the jimmy. The door opened with a loud crack.

The detective entered a darkened room. Waited for his eyes to adjust to the darkness.

"All right, mister," a woman's voice said, "hold it right there."

52

Fourteen

My nephew, Max, is a private detective, too. His girl-friend, a beautiful redhead, is also one. It is beginning to look like a dynasty. One I can support wholeheartedly. Why not? I am the king.

FROM THE CASEBOOKS OF MORRIS WEISS

The detective stood perfectly still and stared into the darkness, waiting for something to take shape. Across the room in a corner by a bookcase he could make out a young woman. As his eyes adjusted, the figure began to take shape, and not an unpleasant one either.

Blond shoulder-length hair, slim figure, lips pouting—in dim light she could easily be mistaken for the movie stars Lizabeth Scott or Lauren Bacall.

Of course, he was no Humphrey Bogart. Then again, Bogart was no real detective.

The woman, naturally enough, held a gun in her hand. Everyone was watching too many movies.

"Okay, mister," she said, "make it quick. Who are you?"

"Morris Weiss, Jake's friend."

"The detective?"

"In the flesh."

"What are you doing here?"

"Looking for Jake."

"He's lost again, ain't he?"

"Something like that."

She stuck the gun in her purse and stepped out of the shadows.

Weiss stared at her.

She's younger than I thought, he realized. *How does Lefkowitz come to a girl like this? Maybe she's looking for a father?*

What he said was, "It is better that he stay lost, Miss Longrin."

"How do ya know my name?"

Weiss smiled.

"It is no secret," he said "Besides, the Butcher's mother told me."

"That old cow?"

He raised an eyebrow.

"You dislike her?"

"She's an old biddy. She oughta learn to mind her own damn business."

"If she had," Weiss said, "I would not be here now."

"Yeah? And—so what?"

She is right, he thought. *I am making a muddle of this.*

"In effect," Weiss said, "I am working for Jake. His newspaper hired me to find him."

"Yeah, yeah, he told me somethin' like that might happen."

Lefkowitz, Weiss mused, *must be smarter than I thought.*

"Jake said he could count on the union to get him outta this mess."

"An optimist," Weiss said. "Did he mention what the mess was?"

"Uh-uh. He told me nothing."

"Miss Longrin—"

"Why don'tcha call me Sally."

"My pleasure, Sally."

"Okay, that's better," said Sally deftly sliding a Kool out of her cigarette case. "Jake told me it was all about some guy called Bernie."

"Ah, the elusive Bernie," Weiss said as he lit her cigarette.

"Yeah, you know him?"

"Not yet. But I will soon enough."

"They are out to get him," she said. "And Jake, too."

"They?"

She shrugged.

"We didn't talk about that," she said.

"I see," Weiss said. "So what did you talk about?"

"Feelings. With a capital *F*."

The detective nodded.

"Do those feelings include Jake's wife?" he heard himself say.

"Uh-uh. She don't count no more."

"How sad for her."

Sally said, "They fell outta love."

"With your help," he said smiling.

"I had nothing to do with it."

The detective shrugged.

"If you say so," he said.

"Damn right I say so. Let's get this straight. I ain't no home wrecker."

"Of course not."

"Say," she said, "you ain't going back to the city soon?"

"I am," Weiss said.

"Take me along, willya? I got a car here. But I don't wanna ride alone."

"Certainly. But what about Jake?"

She put her hands on her hips.

"Enough is enough," she said. "He was supposed to be back inside two hours. What's it now? Six going on seven."

"Follow me," Weiss said.

In a real crisis, the detective thought, *Jake's wife would have waited longer. But this might not be a real crisis, only a waste of my time. Jake seems to have only temporarily disappeared and only to certain people.* Still, Weiss felt vaguely disloyal taking off with this woman. *The job is beginning to get un-*

der my skin. What I should do is go for a vacation af-
ter Lefkowitz turns up. And take Ida with me if she's
free. The idea cheered him.

"Where're you parked?" the girl asked.

"Over there."

But Weiss could no longer see the car. It had begun to snow hard.

The last thing I need is to be snowed in with this
girl.

"You and Jake are planning to get married?" he
said.

"We ain't set a date or nothin'. . . ."

A shot rang out.

The detective, in one motion, fell to the ground,
pulling Sally down with him into the wet snow.

"Lie still!" he whispered urgently.

Half buried in the snow, Weiss reached under his
coat for the Browning and began to shoot back.

They believe I'm Lefkowitz, he thought in dismay.
Imagine taking a bullet for that shlepper. Ida would
never forgive me. I would never forgive me.

"Keep down," Weiss said.

"You don't have to convince me, mister."

"I am glad to see you are a sensible girl."

"Oh yeah, that's me. Sensible Sally. Jake always
said so."

"Excellent. Can you shoot that thing you carry
with you?"

"My gun? Sure. Jake gave it to me."

"Ah."

"But he didn't exactly show me how to use it. I mean I don't really know how it works."

"Don't worry. You are about to learn."

It took the detective only a few moments to show the girl the rudiments of loading, aiming, and firing her pistol. This entire time, the other side kept up a steady barrage of fire, which Weiss returned through the falling snow.

"I'm freezing," the girl complained.

"The lesson is over."

"We can get outta here?"

"Almost."

"Waddya mean 'almost'?"

"You keep them occupied while I crawl over and get behind them."

"Jesus. How do I do that? Maybe a striptease?"

"That will not be necessary. All you do is shoot in their direction."

"What good is that?"

Weiss smiled.

"It gives them something to think about," he said.

"You're outta your mind."

"Not to worry," Weiss said. "I'm very good at this type of work."

"What if you don't come back?"

"I always come back," he said. "Don't waste ammunition. One shot for every five of theirs. understand?"

"What's not to understand?"

"Excellent. When the shooting stops, just jump in your car and drive away from here."

"And leave you behind?"

"Do not worry, Sally. I have my own car."

"Okay," Sally said. "Good luck."

Fifteen

Being the best-dressed man in the room won't help you solve the case, but you'll feel better about having taken it.

FROM THE CASEBOOKS OF MORRIS WEISS

The detective was alone. He didn't mind being alone. Soon he heard Sally returning fire. *Well, at least she's holding to her part of the bargain. Now it is my turn.*

Weiss, keeping very low, crawled off in the snow. *I may be good at this, but it is still hateful.*

It took Weiss, moving very slowly, some ten minutes to reach the roadway. And another three to find the car and get behind it. The car's rear window was totally frosted over. Weiss used his Browning to rap on it. The passenger door popped open and a short man, holding a gun, jumped out into the snow.

"Up with your hands!" the detective yelled. And put three bullets over the man's head.

Close enough to part his hair, Weiss thought.

Then the detective put a bullet through the car's rear window.

The driver had seen enough.

He stepped on the gas and the car skidded and lurched away, churning up a small blizzard behind it. Then it was gone, leaving the two men alone.

The short man seemed torn by indecision.

"You seem to have been deserted, my friend," the detective said, pointing his Browning at the small man.

"Hey, point that thing somewhere else."

"Why were you shooting at us?"

"It wasn't me."

"Then your friend."

"He's no friend. The guy's my boss. There's a difference."

"I'm sure," Weiss said. "And this is about?"

"Some guy called Loft."

"What about him?"

"He knows something he shouldn't."

"And that is?"

"Beats me. I just ride shotgun. No one tells me anything. Why should they? I'm the new guy on the block. Been on the job less than a week."

Weiss considered shooting the man.

"That was the wrong answer," he said, leveling the Browning at his victim.

"Okay, okay, let's not get trigger happy. You can't squeeze blood from a stone, right?"

"You are no stone," Weiss said. "And you will bleed plenty if you do not give me exactly what I want this very second."

"Yeah, I see what you mean."

"That is fortunate," Weiss said, "for you."

"Well, just listen. This Loft guy got Joe mad at him. That's Big Joe, who runs half the numbers on the East Side. Him you know, right?"

"Joe Gold?"

"Yeah, that's the guy."

"I know him," Weiss said, "only by reputation."

"You're lucky. You don't wanna meet up with him in the line of work."

"I'll try and remember that," Weiss said dryly.

"Great. I gave you what you want, right? Now get me outta here."

The detective, after getting the man's name and address from his wallet, left him on a street corner and drove off.

Sixteen

In the old days, the Lower East Side often felt like a small country. A nickel would take you from one end to the other. What a bargain!

FROM THE CASEBOOKS OF MORRIS WEISS

The sky was still overcast the next day. It had been so long since Weiss had seen the sun, he was beginning to wonder if it was still there.

Five stories below, on Grand Street, half the snow was gone, most had turned to slush, and the rest lay in discolored heaps on the curb and in the gutter. He didn't need Ida to remind him to wear his galoshes this morning. In any case, she was off in Philadelphia with her quartet, which didn't prevent him from wishing he was with her now. He put on his black-and-white-striped robe. As was usually the case, he made his own breakfast. Hand-squeezed orange juice, scrambled eggs, a buttered bagel, and two cups of steaming coffee. On the phonograph he had one of the newfangled long-playing records. This one was

Tchaikovsky's violin concerto with Heifetz. *It sounds good. If that doesn't set me up for the day, nothing will.*

He put on a dark-brown tweed jacket, tan slacks, an orange-and-green-striped tie, gray fedora, and a belted tan trench coat. He wrapped his favorite ochre wool scarf around his neck, spent a few seconds admiring himself in the bedroom mirror, decided he liked what he saw, and left the apartment whistling Tchaikovsky.

One hundred and eighty three East Broadway was only a few blocks away.

He walked the short distance, trying to avoid the puddles that had flooded the streets and gutters. At least he knew where he was going, which was more than could be said for those uptown detectives trying to work the Lower East Side.

He passed the Educational Alliance Building, then the small structure housing the Yiddish-language daily *Der Tog* and towering over it the huge *Forverts* Building. He went up the six stone steps, kicked the snow off his galoshes, and entered the large lobby. The elevator was waiting for him, and Alex the operator took him up.

"How are the chess games going, Alex?" Weiss asked.

"At ten cents a game, even the great Capablanca couldn't have made a good living."

Weiss nodded.

"True enough," he said.

"And anyway," Alex said, "most of it I lose at the track."

That was no news. The detective nodded and switched topics.

"Pep," he said, "took back the title from Saddler last week."

"The title," Alex said, "will keep changing hands every time they fight."

"I think so, too," Weiss said. "You went, eh?"

"I always try to, Mr. Weiss. I like the action."

"I went, but I bet on the wrong fellow."

"To me," Alex said, "it happens all the time. And that is why I am still a poor man."

"As long as you know the reason."

Weiss got off at the top floor.

Large letters on the wall said WEVD, which was owned by *The Jewish Daily Forward*.

One happy family, he thought. *They should live so long*.

"I need to see Moisha Solomon," the detective told Julie, the receptionist.

"One moment, Mr. Weiss."

She picked up the phone and in a moment Weiss was seated in Solomon's office in front of his desk.

"So," the station manager said, "what brings you here? Has the Lefkowitz case spilled over to the airwaves?" And he laughed.

Solomon was a tall, heavyset man with a full black mustache. He had been station manager at WEVD for six years. Weiss and he mostly knew each other from the Garden Cafeteria up the block, where many of the *Forverts* staff gathered to eat.

"Maybe it has," Weiss said.

"What are you saying, Morris?"

"There are two men missing from this building, Solomon, and one of them works for your radio station."

Solomon shrugged.

"Do they even know each other?" he said.

"They do."

"How do you know this?"

"I am," Weiss said, "after all, a detective."

Solomon sighed.

"So what do you want from me?" he said.

"Nothing you can't give me."

"That is good to hear. Because my paycheck is already gone."

"Then you are absolutely safe, Solomon."

"So what is it? Quick, before you give me an ulcer."

"Bernard Loft's address and the key to his apartment."

"The address I can easily give you, Weiss."

"But not the key, eh?"

He shrugged.

"Why should he leave his key at the radio station?"

"Then I will settle for the address," Weiss said. "I would also like to see his desk."

"I can assure you, he is not hiding in his desk."

"But maybe something else is," Weiss said.

Seventeen

*The gratifying aspect of my profession is not only solving
a difficult case, but getting the client to pay you on time.
This can be harder than solving the case in the first place.*

FROM THE CASEBOOKS OF MORRIS WEISS

Downstairs in the lobby, the detective put a nickel
in the pay phone, dialed, and waited while the desk
sergeant gave him his party.

"It's Weiss," he said.

"And a good morning to you, Mr. Weiss. What can
I do for you this fine day?"

"Let me take you to brunch, Sergeant O'Toole."

"Ah, the best offer I've had today."

"Probably the only one," Weiss said.

"True, Mr. Weiss, but the day's still young."

"You're right, Sergeant O'Toole. The way this
case is going I'll end up taking you to a late lunch,
too."

"Lunch, too. A red-letter day, and hardly begun."

"It's the Bernard Loft case," Weiss said.

"Ah, that one."

"Another look through your files wouldn't hurt," Weiss said, "if you have the time."

"Of course. Mr. Weiss, what would you say to Ratner's?"

"Ratner's? Excellent. I didn't know you were partial to dairy fare, Sergeant O'Toole."

"I'm not. But Ratner's is on Delancey Street. And so was your Mr. Loft."

"You looked at the Loft file already, eh?"

"An ongoing case, Mr. Weiss. And you and I have been to Ratner's before."

"So we have. Ratner's in twenty minutes?"

"Ratner's in twenty minutes."

An hour and a half later—after a leisurely meal—a squad car pulled up in front of the dairy restaurant, and Weiss and O'Toole climbed in and were carried away.

It was not a long ride. But an uncomfortable one.

The squad car pulled up in front of a tenement on Delancey Street. The three men got out of the car and looked up at the building. A freshly painted green fire escape ran from the fifth to the first floor. Weathered wooden boards comprised the rest of the building. The boards and green fire escape gave the exterior of the house a mismatched appearance.

Mrs. Bloom, the landlady, a short, stout woman in

her midsixties, did not ask to see a search warrant. The two uniforms were more than enough. But she did not have a key to Loft's apartment.

"Don't you worry your head over this," Sergeant O'Toole told her.

"No? How can I not worry?" Mrs. Bloom said, sounding dubious.

"We will take full responsibility," he said.

Weiss gave her his best smile.

"You can rely on him," Weiss said in Yiddish. "Take my word for it."

"I can?" Mrs. Bloom said looking slightly dazed.

"I have known him for years," Weiss said, again in Yiddish.

Sergeant O'Toole stood back and let Weiss do his work. He didn't understand a word of what the private detective was saying. But he had seen the results of these conversations dozens of times in the past. He was quite content to let his friend carry on.

"You are a policeman?" Mrs. Bloom asked.

"No," Weiss said. "But sometimes I work with them."

"Then what are you?"

"I am a private detective."

Mrs. Bloom's hand went to her mouth.

"*Oy vey,*" she said. "You must be Morris Weiss."

"I am."

"It is an honor to meet you, Mr. Weiss."

"The honor is mine, Mrs. Bloom."

She remained standing at her door while the three men went up the stairs.

"What did you tell her, Mr. Weiss?"

"That if she didn't behave, you would arrest her."

"You didn't."

"True," Weiss said smiling. "But I could have."

"Yes," O'Toole said. "If you had suddenly become demented."

The friends laughed. Even Webber, the uniformed officer, smiled.

They reached the third floor.

"It's three-B," O'Toole said.

No more prompting was necessary.

The officer strode to the door and tried the doorknob.

He shook his head.

"Locked," he said.

"You didn't," Weiss asked, "happen to bring along a search warrant, Sergeant O'Toole?"

"Of course I did."

The officer produced a large key ring and began trying keys in the lock.

"Then," Weiss said, "you know a friendly judge."

"All part of this grand job, Mr. Weiss," O'Toole said.

"How do you know him?" Weiss said.

"We went to public school together."

"You don't say?"

A key clicked in the lock. Weiss turned as the door swung open.

The three men hurried into Loft's apartment.

The first thing that Weiss noticed was a shelf of *Ring* magazines, the likes of Joe Louis, Jack Dempsey, Gene Tunny, Joe Walcott, and Tony Zale on the covers. The second thing was in the next room, sticking out of a bedroom closet: a man's head and shoulders.

"Sergeant O'Toole," Weiss called. "Better take a look at this."

"I won't like it, will I?" the sergeant said.

"It's not very likeable," Weiss said.

O'Toole, with Webber at his heels, headed into the bedroom.

"What have we here?" O'Toole said.

"The usual, I'm afraid," Weiss said.

"Not for me," O'Toole said. "It's been a number of years since I met up with a dead customer."

Webber left the room to call it in.

"Get the landlady up here," O'Toole shouted after him. "Know him, Mr. Weiss?"

"I have never laid eyes on him before," he said.

"I'll wager it's this Loft," O'Toole said.

Mrs. Bloom entered the flat, walked into the bedroom, took one glance at what was in the closet, and nearly fainted.

"Do you know this man, Mrs. Bloom?" O'Toole asked.

"I shouldn't know him? He rents this room from me."

"So who is he?" Weiss asked in Yiddish.

"Oy vey," she said. "It is poor Mr. Loft."

Eighteen

Years ago, the mere mention of a Yiddish-speaking private detective would have resulted in derisive laughter. Today, no one knows enough about this issue to even smile. Watch out; the lunatic asylum may be next.

FROM THE CASEBOOKS OF MORRIS WEISS

The morgue wagon had come and gone, taking Loft with it. More police had poured into the small flat. They looked through the closets, drawers, cabinets, under his bed, and in the icebox. They even looked under the green linoleum on the kitchen floor. They found nothing. Weiss stood, hands thrust in his pockets and watched the law at work.

"Mr. Weiss," Sergeant O'Toole said.

"You have found something?"

"Maybe. What do you make of this?"

He handed Weiss a key and a sheet of paper.

Weiss looked at them both.

"They were found in Loft's pocket," O'Toole said.

"Ah-ha," Weiss said.

"Unless I am mistaken, Mr. Weiss, this note should make perfect sense to you. It looks to be in your language."

"You are right, Sergeant O'Toole. Although English, of course, is also my language."

"Of course."

Weiss smiled.

"It says *Loft*," he said.

"The cadaver."

"The very same."

"Anything else?"

"Only that."

"The key, Mr. Weiss, was folded inside this piece of paper."

"Ah, a significant clue, maybe."

"Maybe," O'Toole said. "There is a number on it: three hundred and thirty-four."

"And this means what?"

"Unless I miss my guess, Mr. Weiss, this is a key from a locker in Penn Station."

"You are entrusting this valuable clue to me?"

"For a few days."

"I am honored, Sergeant."

O'Toole smiled.

"If all goes well, Mr. Weiss, you can always take me to dinner. I may even be tax deductible by this time."

"An excellent idea," Weiss said.

"I thought so myself," O'Toole said, beaming.

"Even if this isn't a clue," Weiss said, "I can still take you to dinner."

"What a grand country this is," O'Toole said.

Nineteen

I was something of a pioneer as a Yiddish-speaking private detective. I figured this out when I realized my closest friend in the business was a police sergeant who was Irish and did not speak a word of Yiddish, despite our long years of association.

FROM THE CASEBOOKS OF MORRIS WEISS

Penn Station was its usual dark, cavernous, and echoing self. The odor that Weiss unmistakably associated with train stations saturated the walls and floor. It was well before rush hour and not many commuters were there. Weiss found the locker on the lower level and opened the small metal door with the key. He reached inside and removed a package wrapped in plain brown paper The detective looked at it quizzically. *That was easy*, he thought. *Maybe too easy.* He slipped the package into his coat pocket. This was not the place to start fiddling with packages. Especially one he knew nothing about.

Morris Weiss moved toward the stairs.

"Hey, mister."

Weiss was the only mister around.

He turned in the direction of the voice, which belonged to a large stooped man in a seedy brown overcoat and baggy hat that made him blend perfectly with the brown walls of his surroundings.

It did not cheer Weiss to see this man.

"What do you want?" he said. As if Weiss didn't know. Handout was written all over him.

The large man moved closer to Weiss.

Too close.

Maybe, the detective thought, *it isn't just a handout he wants.*

"Look, mister," he said, "I'm way down on my luck."

This is obvious, the detective thought. *And hardly to your credit.* But he said nothing.

"Can you help me out?"

"How much do you need?" Weiss asked.

He was actually curious.

The man smiled. It was not a nice smile. Which, as it turned out, was a clear mistake. For it warned Weiss that something unpleasant was about to happen.

The detective took immediate steps to assure that the unpleasant thing didn't happen to him but happened instead to the man in the soiled brown overcoat. He removed his hands from his pockets, turned his left shoulder slightly, spread his feet, balled his hands into fists, and waited for the next development.

"How much you got, buddy?"

Here it comes, Weiss thought.

"Too much for you," Weiss said.

"Keep it," the man said.

"That's very kind of you," Weiss said, somewhat surprised.

"Yeah, I'll take that package you got instead." The man rose to his full height.

"What package?"

"The one in your coat pocket, buddy."

Weiss removed the package from his pocket, held it aloft in his right hand.

"This one?" he asked.

The man, never taking his eyes off the prize, reached for it.

Because of their difference in height, the man was no doubt convinced he had an overwhelming advantage—a simple mugging, painless to him, if not to the victim.

In this, like many before him, he was wrong.

And he had managed to irritate the detective in the process.

Weiss let fly a sharp left to the jaw. The same one that had won him many bouts in the days when he was a amateur pugilist. Dropping the package, he followed up with a right cross and a quick left hook.

The detective was considering where else to hit the big man when he obligingly fell down.

Weiss looked down at him, shrugged, and picked up the package. He still had no idea what it contained. Something worth fighting for obviously.

He walked to a phone booth some yards away.

Inside, he quickly sat down and waited.

Someday, he thought, *Ida will happen by and catch me like this. I will have to explain that it is all part of the job. And I am not looking for dropped nickels. A good thing she is a trusting soul.*

Outside, the big man came to his senses slowly, looked around as if amazed to find he was not in his own bed. A few people went by. No one paid the least attention to the fallen man. For once Weiss did not mind the public's indifference. His assailant finally made it to all fours and then was able to stand upright by leaning against the wall.

Serves him right, Weiss thought, *for picking on a smaller man.*

The man pushed off from the wall and began to stagger away. As if gravity had become a spiteful foe clinging to his legs.

The detective saw that he no longer needed the cover of the phone booth, and followed at a discreet distance. They left Penn Station, wound their way through the half-empty streets. The man turned into a tavern on Eighth Avenue. Weiss did not want to spend the day watching his assailant getting drunk. A phone booth was up the block. The detective went to it, stepped in, and depositing a nickel, dialed Boris Minsky.

"Boris," Weiss said. "I'm glad you're home."

"Mr. Weiss," Minsky said.

"No, no, Boris. Not Mr. Weiss. Morris, please. I thought we had an agreement."

"Of course . . . Morris."

"Very good, Boris. You are making progress."

"Thank you," Minsky said. "Although Morris and Boris do sound like a vaudeville act."

"If it is our act," Weiss said, "it will be a great one."

"That is good to hear."

"I have a job for you, Boris."

"That is also good to hear."

"Excellent. Meet me at Twenty-eighth Street and Eighth Avenue as soon as you can. Across the street from the celebrated Green Shamrock Tavern."

"I have never heard of it," Minsky said.

"Neither have I," Weiss said. "Let us hope it lives up to its reputation."

"What reputation?"

"Detective O'Toole," Weiss said, "speaks very highly of it. And he is a connoisseur."

"He is the one who celebrates it?"

"Whenever he can."

An hour later, the detective and his assistant were strolling after the tall man in the direction of Fourteenth Street.

Minsky said, "He is not distinguishing himself as a walker."

Weiss shrugged. "He has had a difficult day."

They followed the large man to a tenement on Fourteenth Street near Seventh Avenue, and stood across the street as a light snapped on in one of the front windows on the second floor.

"That must be him," Minsky said.

Weiss said, "Wait here"

He went across to the tenement, tried the front door, and finding it unlocked, entered.

He returned to Boris in less than four minutes.

"Sound asleep," he said. "Room three-C. His name is Joe Lansing according to his ID."

"You looked in his wallet?"

"Of course."

"What if he woke up?"

The detective shrugged.

"I would have," he said, "put him to sleep again. Go up and get a look at him. By tonight I will have sent a replacement for you. Be back here by eight in the morning to take over. This job pays double."

"Why, is it dangerous?"

"Not more than usual, Boris. This fellow has no idea who you are, or that we are on to him. And the printers have a large war chest. It was put aside for strikes. At first I didn't want to touch it, but when are there strikes at the *Forverts*? So the war chest will pay us to find their missing colleague. It is a good cause."

"I never doubted it," Minsky said.

"Good," Weiss said.

"The last thing I want to do," Minsky said, "is bite the hand that feeds me."

"Your mastery of American idiom does you credit, Boris."

"You are pulling my leg," Minsky said.

Weiss laughed.

"You are well on your way," he said, "to becoming a bona fide American private detective."

"Is that all it takes?"

"Actually," Weiss said, "it takes a bit more."

"So?"

Weiss smiled.

"In this country," he said, "appearance is half the battle."

"So you have often said."

"Because it is true," the detective said.

"The pursuit of truth is its own virtue."

"Then you will be a very virtuous man," Weiss said smiling.

"That was always my hope," Minsky said.

"Just remember to use those special words regularly and you will sound just like a private detective."

"But you do not use them yourself."

"I don't have to," Weiss said. "I *am* a private detective."

Twenty

—◆▪◆❈◆▪◆—

*Sam Spade and Philip Marlowe would have had a hard
time on the Lower East Side without a good translator,
one trusted and respected by the community. Naturally, I
know just the man for the job. But frankly, I would much
rather solve my own cases.*

FROM THE CASEBOOKS OF MORRIS WEISS

A few blocks south of Penn Station, Weiss remembered the package in his coat pocket. He shook his
head. *I'd better marry Ida while I still remember
what a good idea it is*, he thought. *If I'm this forgetful at twenty-nine, what will I be like when I'm
thirty-nine?*

He sighed.

And turned in at the first bar he came to.

It was empty at this hour, which did not bother
Weiss at all. He preferred restaurants to bars anyway.
Wine with dinner rather than hard liquor. And if it
had to be a bar, one in which he felt at home and was
known to the proprietor and some of the other customers.

This was not such a bar, but it would do quite well for what he had in mind. And luckily he would be here for only a short while.

He chose a corner table, ordered a beer on tap, and opened the package.

Like the bar, the package was empty, too.

Well, he thought, *along with my mind, that makes it a clean sweep.*

Weiss sipped his beer and carefully examined the brown wrapping paper for clues. There were none. The white cardboard box which had been inside the paper was also devoid of clues. And empty. This certainly made no sense. The thing to do if he wanted some answers was to make his questions official. He went to the phone booth at the other end of the bar and gave the phone company its nickel. Soon he was on the line to Sergeant O'Toole.

"Mr. Weiss, I'll wager something of interest has happened since last we met."

"You'd win that wager, too."

"And it was?"

"I was almost mugged this afternoon."

"You?"

Weiss sighed. "It's true."

"Almost, is it?"

"Yes."

"You didn't put the unfortunate fellow in the hospital, Mr. Weiss?"

"I wanted to," Weiss said, "but the man fell down before I could do a good job of it. His name is Joe Lansing."

Weiss gave the sergeant the tenement's address and room number.

"You might want to look in on him," he said.

"I just might at that, Mr. Weiss."

"You never know what you will find."

"If it leads to fame and fortune, Mr. Weiss, I will certainly remember you."

"That is very kind of you, Sergeant. But I expected nothing less."

Both men laughed.

Twenty-one

It is better to be poor and honest than rich and a crook. I have heard this said often. But I have never figured out why. Probably because it sounds so nice. Nicer would be rich and honest. This they could put to music.

FROM THE CASEBOOKS OF MORRIS WEISS

"Who is joking?" Weiss said.

"Ha!" Ida said. "You are always joking."

The detective shrugged.

"Well," Weiss said, "there I was on my hands and knees in a phone booth in Penn Station waiting for this large fellow who I had knocked cold as a mackerel to come to, when who should suddenly, out of the blue, pop into my head but . . ."

"A piece of strudel?"

"That would be into my mouth," Weiss said.

"An old girlfriend?"

"My best girlfriend," Weiss said. And put his arm around her.

"That must be me!" Ida said.

"Who else?" Weiss said.

They were in Weiss's place on Grand Street, in Weiss's bed. A half-empty bottle of wine sat on the night table along with two glasses. Steam hissed from the radiator, which occasionally clanged. Ida's apartment, in the East Fifties, was more to Weiss's liking. But it was in the wrong place for what he had to do that day. They had been here for over three hours, and busy for most of the time. He, at the moment, in his striped cotton pajamas and she in her silk flower-print nightgown. They embraced, stared into each other's eyes, and were moving even closer when the phone rang.

"Don't go away," Weiss said.

"Where am I going in my nightgown?" Ida asked.

"Whoever it is," Weiss said, "I will shoot them the first chance I get. Hello," he said into the receiver.

"Mr. Weiss . . ."

"Boris, is that you?"

"Yes, Mr. Weiss," Minsky said.

"Don't shoot Boris," Ida called from the bed. "I like him."

"You have been spared," Weiss said. "She likes you."

"That is always a comfort."

"But not for long if you keep calling me *Mr. Weiss*."

"I shall banish it from my lips."

"That would be very nice," Weiss said. "What is the trouble?"

"The man in room three-C," Minsky said. "Two men came for him."

"He went away with them?"

"Not willingly," Minsky said. "They dragged him out."

"You are on the street now?"

"I am."

"Do you see them anywhere?"

"No. They have just turned a corner."

"How far away?"

"Two blocks."

"Did you bring a gun?"

"I do not even own a gun," Minsky said. "Unless you mean my dueling pistols."

"Forget the dueling pistols," Weiss said. "These fellows are not gentlemen. Which way did they head, Boris?"

"West."

"Excellent. I will call Sergeant O'Toole and arrange for a patrol car to pick us both up. If we find him and his abductors, they will all be rattled. Maybe we will learn something."

"I am rattled myself," Boris said.

"A few more cases like this under your belt and you will be an experienced professional."

"Like you?"

"Well, maybe not exactly like me," Weiss said.

Twenty-two

Yes, it is possible to have a very big money case on the Lower East Side. Like a lot of things in life—it just isn't very likely.

FROM THE CASEBOOKS OF MORRIS WEISS

Not one but three patrol cars showed up. A glowing testament to Sergeant O'Toole's growing authority in the department. *I picked the right friend years ago,* Weiss thought happily.

He was already downstairs on the street when they arrived.

The private detective climbed into the backseat of the first patrol car and glanced behind him at the other two.

"What has become of my colleague Minsky?" he asked.

"Not to worry, sir," the driver said. "A car was dispatched some five minutes ago. He should be cruising into the neighborhood by now."

"All right then," Weiss said. "Uptown toward Fourteenth Street near Eighth Avenue. And step on it."

The detective grinned.

He had first heard the expression on the radio program *Gangbusters* when he visited his friend Feldman, and his two sons had neglected to close the bedroom door. Which was often.

He had always wanted to say that, but had never had the opportunity before. Then he stopped grinning, remembering Ida's expression when he left. *I will make it up to her,* he vowed. *And to myself, too.* It would not be easy. Unless he caught a master criminal with a big reward on his head. Then of course he could take Ida on a round-the-world cruise. Alas, the man he knocked out was no master criminal. If there was a master criminal involved, this was the fellow who shined his shoes.

The patrol car meanwhile headed north on Sixth Avenue.

Weiss peered hopefully out the windows at the passing cars, but saw no one who looked even vaguely familiar.

What am I doing here? By now, Ida has no doubt returned to her own apartment. A wasted opportunity for us to be together. Weiss sighed. *When will I be able to choose pleasure over business? Maybe Rockefeller will hire me to oversee his security staff?*

As if the gods had instantly decided to prove him

wrong, a voice sounded over the car radio announcing that two men who fit the suspects' descriptions were seen in a black Ford heading south on Tenth Avenue, a street given over to vacant lots, some billboards advertising Camel cigarettes, Duz and Oxydol laundry soaps, and a few dilapidated tenements that were barely standing and even gave Weiss the shivers. It was a great place to avoid.

As if reading his thoughts, the driver stepped on the gas.

"Hang on, Mr. Weiss," the driver told him. And hit the siren.

From the distance, the detective heard other sirens as though in answer to their own.

He settled back in his seat, crossed one leg over the other so as not to damage the crease in his pants, and let the coppers carry the ball for a while. Of course, he now owed O'Toole another dinner. But it was worth it. He didn't get to ride in a patrol car every day chasing after lowlifes. And, aside from the invaluable help he often gave him, Weiss always enjoyed the sergeant's company.

He had first met the Irishman when he was still walking a beat on the Lower East Side, and Weiss, in his late teens, was an unbeaten amateur boxer. O'Toole, who followed the fights, had seen him in the ring and liked what he saw. He dropped around one night after a fight to let him know. The pair had hit it off from the very start and remained friends through the years. It was a friendship that had paid off for both of them.

His patrol car meanwhile had begun to skillfully maneuver through traffic and before Weiss knew it was on Tenth Avenue and Eighteenth Street.

Where the detective was greeted by a very pleasing sight.

A black Ford stood abandoned in the middle of the street not two blocks away, patrol cars blocking it front and back.

Two men were running on the sidewalk.

Catch them in your headlights," he told the driver, "if you can."

"Sure, I can," he said.

The driver sped up, and for a brief moment Weiss got a nice view of their profiles—sharp features, high cheekbones, clean-shaven jaws—which the detective promptly tried to commit to memory. Dunninger the mentalist, of radio fame, would have done a better job. But for Weiss this would have to do.

The pair ducked down Fifteenth Street, five of New York's finest on their heels.

For policemen, they run like athletes, Weiss thought. *Even for athletes, they run like athletes.*

Then he noticed someone he had at first overlooked.

Standing by a lamppost, as if trying to wish himself into invisibility, was Joe Lansing. A policeman stood next to him.

Weiss was content to sit this one out. So, apparently, were his police escorts. He would buy Ida the biggest bunch of flowers she had ever seen. If that didn't do it, he would think of something else.

He always did. And it was always a pleasure.

Twenty-three

As a private detective you get to meet a lot of interesting people. The trouble is, half of them are crooks. This isn't so bad if you keep a sharp eye on your wallet.

FROM THE CASEBOOKS OF MORRIS WEISS

"No, I didn't know them guys from a hole in the wall."

"But you took the job?" the police detective said.

"Sure I took the job. It was easy money," Joe Lansing said.

"What made it so easy?" the police detective said.

"They told me the guy was a pushover."

"Was he?"

"Uh-uh."

"Did they tell you who he was?"

"No."

"So what *did* they tell you, Joe?"

"To hang around this locker at Penn Station."

"And did you?"

"Yeah."

"For how long?"

"Three days."

"Pretty long time."

"Not so long. The pay was okay."

"And then?"

"Someone showed up, this guy."

And the man pointed at Weiss, across the table.

"I admit it is true," Weiss said, a smile on his face.

"They told me the guy would take somethin' outta the locker."

"And did he?"

"Yeah."

"What was it?"

"A package."

"Know what was in it?"

"Beats me."

"They didn't tell you?"

He shrugged. "Why should they?" he said.

"What were you supposed to do?"

"Take it away from him."

"How?"

"Slug him."

"Just like that?"

"They said he was a pushover."

"Was he?"

"Uh-uh."

"What happened?"

"He slugged *me*."

The officer nodded.

"Okay, Joe." he said. "We need something from you now."

"Like what?"

"We need you to testify," the police detective said.

"Yeah? About what?"

"The pair who hired you."

"Why would I do that?"

"To stay out of the clink."

"Forget it, pal."

"You want to go to jail?"

"You get a load of them guys?"

"So?"

"What I wanna do is to go on livin'."

"They didn't look like much," the police detective said.

"Try 'em in a dark alley, pal."

"All right, Joe. You've had your chance."

"Some chance."

Twenty-four

It's nice being your own boss. The problem is that the boss is always broke at the same time you are.

FROM THE CASEBOOKS OF MORRIS WEISS

Weiss identified himself for the front desk sergeant. "I would like to speak with the two men who were brought in late last night," he said.

The detective was enjoying himself. The police had conveniently run down the pair of lowlifes he was after. Now all he had to do was interview them. Child's play.

The sergeant, a big jowly man, shook his head.

"Sorry," he said. "They're gone. Both of 'em."

Morris Weiss made a face.

"They escaped?"

"They were sprung, brother."

"When?"

The sergeant looked down at his ledger.

"'Bout an hour ago."

"Fast work. Who stood bail?"

"Fletcher and Steel."

"I know the names," Weiss said. "But that's all."

"Big outfit. Judge Brisken," the sergeant said, "called in very early to arrange it."

"That was nice of him," the detective said.

"Nothing special," the clerk said. "The judge does it all the time."

"These two had names?"

"Sure. Harry Sable and Victor Norris."

"Thank you," Morris Weiss said.

"Feldman?"

"Morris, is that you?"

"None other," Weiss said. "Why do you ask?"

"The connection is bad," Feldman said.

"I am making this call from the hoosegow. What can you expect?"

"You are a prisoner, Morris, or what?"

"I am only passing through."

"Ah," Feldman said, "too bad. I was hoping to finally stand by your side in court and show you what I can do."

"I already know what you can do. Your clients are still sitting here from the last time I visited."

Feldman sighed. "You know what it is, Morris? You get used to a place, you don't want to leave it."

Both men laughed.

"So," Weiss said. "What can you tell me about Fletcher and Steel?"

"The lawyers?"

"Who else?"

"What's to tell? They represent crooks, Morris. Probably they themselves are crooks."

"I wanted a word with two lowlifes here, but Fletcher and Steel beat me to it."

"They came themselves?"

"I don't think so, Feldman. They would have had to come here too early. *I* had to come here too early."

"You are right, Morris. What is the use of being a boss if you have to work like a hired hand?"

"What do you know about a Judge Brisken?"

"Brisken? Him I try to avoid at all costs."

"Then I will follow your example, Feldman."

"Of course, Morris. That's what friends are for."

Weiss hung up smiling, reached into a coat pocket, and came up with another nickel. *Without all these nickels*, he thought, *I would need a flock of carrier pigeons. The birdseed alone would ruin me.*

Twenty-five

If crime doesn't pay, why are there so many lawyers? I always ask this question. Even good lawyers don't have a good answer. In fact, they don't want one. It's enough to keep stuffing big bills into their pockets.

FROM THE CASEBOOKS OF MORRIS WEISS

He dialed the second number quickly from memory. The phone was picked up on the first ring.

"Orchard Street Bakery," Itchy, the co-owner, said.

Weiss identified himself.

"Mr. Weiss. A good thing you called. Yossel has this very moment taken from the oven some very nice challah."

"Yossel makes more than very nice challah," Weiss said.

"So what does he make?"

"Outstanding challah," the detective said.

"You are right, Mr. Weiss. I am sending you over a loaf right now. Hot from the oven."

Itchy, Benjy, and their coworkers were at one time part of the notorious Odessa Gangsters. Then they came to America and found to their surprise that here in the "golden land" they could earn more going straight. Itchy and Benjy had become partners in the Orchard Street Bakery—a sort of landmark now for old-time Odessa toughs who had settled on Manhattan's Lower East Side. Itchy and Benjy were out of the robbery business, but they still did favors for their friends. Morris Weiss was one of these.

"Right now, unfortunately, I am not at home," Weiss said.

"I am sorry," Itchy said.

"Not as sorry as I am," Weiss said. "My mouth is already watering."

"I will make it up to you, Mr. Weiss."

"Sooner than you think, Itchy. I have a job for you."

"What? A wedding, a birthday, a bar mitzvah?"

Weiss said, "Not that kind of a job. What you used to do in the old country."

"Really?"

"Absolutely."

"Then not on the phone. We must get together."

"Say in an hour at the bakery."

"Good. We have a room in back."

"Have Benjy join us."

"Benjy? It is that kind of a job, eh?"

"Exactly," Morris Weiss said.

Twenty-six

Even a private detective is never very private. He is acquainted with a number of policemen, thugs, and other lowlifes. The police are usually the best of the lot—but not always.

FROM THE CASEBOOKS OF MORRIS WEISS

He dialed again.

"Mr. Weiss," Sergeant O'Toole said. "It's good to hear from you. How are you?"

"I could be worse," Weiss said, "and probably will be if—"

"If what, Mr. Weiss?"

"I can't get the information I'm looking for."

"This is something I can assist you with?"

"It is."

"Then out with it, Mr. Weiss."

"The pair of thugs you had your men pick up for me were in your lockup this morning. Sometime around seven-thirty."

"You helped put them there, of course?"

"Only false modesty could make me deny it.

Although all I did was encourage your men from the backseat of their patrol car."

O'Toole laughed.

"An affliction," he said, "with which you are totally unacquainted, eh?"

"Totally. Unfortunately, I know almost nothing about them except their names."

"Hold on, Mr. Weiss. That can be remedied."

"That's good," Weiss said.

"I'll be back before you know it," O'Toole said.

Weiss remained standing in the corridor with the receiver pressed to his ear. He smelled Lysol, heard clanging cell doors, and the raised voices of prisoners. It was not his favorite place. Also, as usual, there were at least three radios playing simultaneously, each tuned to a different station. He recognized in this jumble only one voice, that of the nutritionist Carlton Fredericks, whom Ida followed faithfully. And through Ida, Weiss did, too.

Who would be listening to him in this place?

The detective sighed.

Better not to know. It will only haunt me.

Presently the sergeant returned with a pair of names.

"Sable and Norris, Mr. Weiss, are freelance petty criminals. They get picked up at least once a week on minor charges, but have done very little jail time."

"Judge Brisken?"

"A distinct possibility."

"Fletcher and Steel?"

"No doubt about it."

The detective asked for and received the addresses of both thugs.

"What do these two do," Weiss said, "when they're not breaking the law?"

"They are always breaking the law," O'Toole said. "Otherwise, they work as meatpackers." He gave Weiss the location of the plant. And the two men said their goodbyes. Then Weiss all but ran from the place.

Twenty-seven

Lowlifes shoot first and ask questions later—if the victim is still alive. Private detectives can't do that. What they can do is shoot straighter than the lowlifes and duck at the appropriate time. This I have been doing for years now. I attribute my longevity to it and the consumption of fresh fruits and vegetables.

FROM THE CASEBOOKS OF MORRIS WEISS

"This way," Weiss told the boy from the Fifty-fifth Street Lexington Avenue Flower Shop. And led him up the hallway. Their footsteps were muffled by the thick brown carpet on the floor. But not the sound of Ida practicing her viola. It brought a smile to the detective's face. And almost tears to his eyes. He had an urge to stop and just listen quietly before announcing his presence. But the boy from the flower shop would get into trouble if he spent too much time here. The detective didn't want that. He halted in front of the door, rang the bell, stepped aside, and let the boy take his place. The bouquet of flowers was so immense that the boy was all but lost behind it.

The detective began to question the wisdom of so many flowers.

The door opened. And a dumbfounded Ida stared at the profusion of flowers.

"You have the right apartment?" she asked.

The delivery boy grinned, nodded toward the detective.

"Compliments of Mr. Morris Weiss," he said, placing the monstrous bouquet on the floor.

"Ah, it becomes clear now," Ida said with a grin.

The boy turned, winked at Weiss, tipped his cap to Ida, pocketed the five-dollar tip he had just been handed. Then nonchalantly strolled toward the stairs, as though such things happened every day.

"I have just given him a month's wages," Weiss said.

"Yours or his?" Ida asked.

"His," the detective said. "Fortunately."

Weiss stepped over to Ida, wrapped his arms around her, and gave her a long and ardent kiss. They disentangled. And Ida sighed.

"Just step one," Weiss said.

"Step one of what, Moisheleh?"

"My atonement."

"So what's step two?"

"What we were interrupted doing yesterday."

"Oh," Ida said. *"That."*

"Of course. What else?"

With one hand gently squeezing Ida's shoulder and the other dragging the bouquet, Weiss entered the apartment.

"How long do we have?" she asked.

"Until after nightfall, Idaleh."

"That much?" she said.

"Maybe even more."

"What a treat," she said.

"We would have much more if it wasn't for this business with the lowlifes."

"Moisheleh, you make your living from lowlifes."

"Catching them. There is a big difference."

"And if there were no lowlifes?"

"I could always be a boxer."

"Really?"

"Why not? I was undefeated as an amateur."

"Moisheleh, have you seen what they look like later in life?"

Weiss smiled.

"Not to worry," he said. "I am safe. There will always be lowlifes. It is, alas, the way of the world."

Twenty-eight

The last thing the lowlifes will expect is a capable Yiddish private detective. It will throw them off guard. And make it that much easier to mop up with them.

FROM THE CASEBOOKS OF MORRIS WEISS

Morris Weiss, hands in overcoat pockets, smiled up at Benjy.

"Whatever you do," he said, "do not hurt them."

"Never," Benjy said. "Even when I worked in the kosher slaughterhouse in Odessa, the cows would line up to be slaughtered by me."

Itchy smiled.

"He has been telling this story for years," he said.

"Now I am worried," Weiss said.

And all three laughed.

The three men stood on the corner of Fourteenth Street and Seventh Avenue. All three wore long woolen coats. Weiss and Itchy wore gray fedoras, Benjy a green checkered peaked cap. A foghorn sounded from somewhere on the Hudson. Vacant lots surrounded them. One lone factory could be seen off in the distance. A billboard advertising Thom Mc-Cann shoes. An icy wind had started to blow in from the waterfront, making it feel even colder.

"A good night to stay home, eh?" Itchy said.

"As long," Benjy said, "as our friends don't feel the same way."

"They bunk together?" Itchy said.

Weiss nodded.

The detective thought of Ida and realized there were better ways to spend the night. Of course, this was hardly news.

It had begun to lightly snow when Weiss spied two moving figures up the block.

"I think," he said, "they may be coming."

"You're not sure?" Itchy said.

Weiss shrugged.

"Who can be sure of anything?" he said.

"We need a detective here," Itchy said, "not a philosopher."

"If they reach for guns," Weiss said, "we'll know they are guilty of something. Also remember to duck. That is all the detective wisdom I have tonight."

"It is all that is needed," Benjy said.

The three men stepped away from the street lamp's glare, each moving in a different direction.

They stood waiting quietly in the darkness.

The two men were almost abreast of the lamppost when the detective called out their names.

"Up with your hands," he said.

Itchy and Benjy said the very same thing from their respective positions.

Sable went for his gun.

Benjy seemed to step out of nowhere. His big hand closed over the gun, removed it effortlessly from the smaller man's grip, and tossed it to the pavement. He grabbed Sable or Norris, Weiss couldn't yet tell which one, and hoisted him above his head. Then, feetfirst, slammed him down to the pavement. Weiss had seen Benjy perform this feat at least three times, but never ceased to marvel at it. Usually it discouraged all resistance. The other man had turned, no doubt to run, when the detective shouted, "Don't move!" By then Weiss had his Browning high-powered revolver in his hand. The manufacturer had named it "the Captain." And for good reason. The Captain commanded respect. Weiss put a bullet over the fleeing man's head, which stopped him dead in his tracks.

He spun around, hands raised.

"Waddya want?" he said.

"Who is Sable and who is Norris?" Weiss said.

"He's Sable," the shorter of the two said.

"Making you Norris, eh?" Weiss said.

"Sure," Norris said. "Norris, that's me. Waddya want?"

"All right," the detective said. "You men do what?"

"We don't," Norris said.

"Unemployed," Sable said, sounding very sad.

"Where do you live?"

"Brooklyn Men's Shelter," Norris said.

"You two are a long way from home," Weiss said.

"Lookin' for work," Norris said.

"Times are hard," Sable said. "Very hard."

At ten at night? These fakers are fooling no one, Weiss thought. He said, "They are about to get harder."

He nodded to Itchy.

"Who's to know if we kill 'em?" Itchy said. He took out a long-barreled revolver and aimed it at the pair.

"Into the alley widdya!" he yelled.

"Hey," Norris yelled. "You crazy?!"

Benjy glowered at the pair, flexed his fingers meaningfully, and took a step forward. Like a man who delighted in his nefarious work. Or someone who had seen one too many monster movies.

"You're right," the detective said. "Better kill them, I think."

"Hold on," Sable yelled.

"Not so fast!" Norris shouted.

"Too late," Benjy said.

Twenty-nine

The job of the Yiddish private detective is to save the un-worldly from themselves and from the lowlifes. First it is necessary to make sure that the victim believes you and is ready to hire you—or you will be working for nothing. There is no future in that. Don't do it.

FROM THE CASEBOOKS OF MORRIS WEISS

Benjy grabbed Norris and lifted him off the ground by the front of his coat.

"I bang you headfirst into the ground."

Sable tried to run.

Itchy jumped him and put a strong forearm around the man's neck.

Sable said something that sounded like *"Gaak!"*

"I warned you," Weiss said. "I cannot control them. They are insane."

"T'hell with this shit," Norris yelled. "Waddya want to know?"

"Yeah," Sable said, rubbing his neck. "Ask us anything! We ain't paid enough to put our lives on the line."

113

"That is sensible," Weiss said. 'I would not want you on my conscience."

"I still bang them headfirst in the ground?" Benjy asked hopefully, still doing his imitation of a lunatic.

"Later," Itchy said.

"If they misbehave," Weiss said.

If they only knew this giant makes the best cupcakes on the Lower East Side, they would have tossed down their guns willingly, Weiss thought. *Maybe they did know but ignored it. What can you expect from lowlifes?*

"Who told you to kidnap Joe Lansing?" the detective said.

"The foreman," Norris said.

"At the meatpacking plant?"

"Yeah, he told us to snatch the guy."

"He is your boss?"

"Sure. He gives us jobs that don't got nothin' to do with meat."

"What did he want from Lansing?"

"A package."

Ah, the famous empty package.

"What was supposed to be in it?"

"He didn't say."

"This foreman, he has a name?"

"Sure. Bill."

"Just Bill?"

"Lazio. Bill Lazio."

"And the plant is where?"

"It's in the Bronx."

"It has no address, eh?"

Weiss was given a Hunts Point address.

"Where can I find this Lazio?" Weiss said.

"The plant," Sable said.

"Now?" Weiss said.

"Sure," Sable said. "He works the night shift."

"Okay," Weiss said. "Beat it."

The hoodlums did not have to be told twice. Turning on their heels, they all but flew up the street. They did not look back.

The three men stood and watched them go.

Benjy finally spoke.

"Why did you do this, Morris?" he said.

"Do what?"

"Let them go."

The detective shrugged.

"Why not?" he said.

"He *always* has a good reason," Itchy said. "What did I tell you?"

Weiss smiled.

"It is an excellent thing to let them go," Weiss said. "Or we would be stuck with them. Am I right?"

"He's right," Benjy said. "I think."

"Thank you," Weiss said.

The three men began strolling back toward Eighth Avenue.

"There is an automat," Weiss said. "We can stop

for a coffee and a piece of pie. Also, I have a phone call to make."

"And then?" Benjy said.

"Drive on to the plant," Weiss said. "What else?"

"I am glad," Itchy said, "you know what you are doing. Someone should know."

"True," Weiss said. "Better me than a stranger, eh?"

Thirty

*It is often a good thing to have some trusted friends cover-
ing your back, as lowlifes have been known to shoot first
and think later. This is because they are very stupid. Better they should get shot than you. Who, after all, is going
to miss a lowlife?*

FROM THE CASEBOOKS OF MORRIS WEISS

"You want what?"

"To know what happened to Jake Lefkowitz," Weiss said.

"Never heard of him."

"What about Sable and Norris? You are Bill Lazio?"

"Yeah, so what?"

"You *are* their foreman, Mr. Lazio," Weiss said.

"That's a lie!"

The detective and his two friends exchanged glances.

They were standing in the very small, dark office of the foreman, Bill Lazio, a short, corpulent man of about fifty.

Outside it was still snowing lightly.

Weiss was relieved he could not hear the cries of

animals being slaughtered. Of course, this was only a meatpacking plant, not a slaughterhouse. Still, the connection between the two made the detective feel slightly uneasy. *As though I didn't already have enough to worry about. Now my mind is occupied with lambs and cows. But at least not pigs. They will have to worry about themselves.*

Lazio rose from behind his desk.

"I don't gotta listen to this garbage!" he yelled. "Get out! I'm busy. I don't got time for this."

"Very well," Weiss said. "We will be going."

"Damn straight," the foreman said. "And don't come back!"

"But we *will* be back," Weiss said.

"Then I'll be waiting for you!" Lazio said, shaking his fist.

But the detective and his two friends had already turned their backs and were out the door.

In the hallway, Weiss switched to Yiddish. And began walking very fast.

"What's the hurry?" Itchy said.

"We are in enemy territory. He may have a dozen men at his disposal."

"Since when," Benjy said, "are we afraid of a mere dozen men?"

"We're not," Weiss said.

"So?" Benjy said.

"It would help our cause," Weiss said, "if they thought we were terrified."

"That," Itchy said, "may be asking too much."

His two friends, though taller, had to hurry to keep up with him.

Weiss had his Browning out. The other two also had their guns in their hands, hanging at their sides. All they needed was someone to shoot at. Weiss figured they might have that soon enough. But he was in no hurry to dodge bullets.

"So, how did it go?" he said.

"Well, you convinced me," said Itchy.

"Of what?"

"That you are a troublemaker."

Weiss said, "I *am* a troublemaker. When it is called for."

"You should have let me kill him," Benjy said.

"Like in Odessa, eh?"

"He never killed anyone in Odessa," Itchy said, "except in self-defense."

"And you did?" Benjy said.

By then they had reached the outside, and were running for Weiss's black Packard parked near the side of the building.

The detective pulled out his car key and opened the driver's door. The coast was still clear. The three men climbed into the car.

And they took off.

Thirty-one

My nephew and I run the same type of agency now that I did then. It is one with menschlichkeit. If you don't know the meaning of that word, don't worry about it. We do. And that's what counts.

FROM THE CASEBOOKS OF MORRIS WEISS

Hunts Point, at this time, was mainly an undeveloped stretch of land in the Bronx. The meatpacking plant, a five-story concrete block, stood in near isolation among bare, snow-covered trees and bushes. Icy pavement ran to and from the plant. A garage sat at its back door. A sole billboard across the street said, "Smoke Old Gold Cigarettes." It was decorated with the head of a blonde puffing at a cigarette. Weiss noted her brilliant white teeth. *Not for long*, he thought.

A black touring car shot out of the garage and turned in the direction of the Packard.

"Ah-ha," Weiss said.

"About time," Itchy said.

"I was starting to fall asleep," Benjy said.

"This should wake you up," the detective said.

Weiss pressed down on the gas. The Packard glided into the darkness.

"Hold on," Weiss said.

"Some car, Morris," Benjy said.

"I agree with you," the detective said. "Now watch this."

The car behind them seemed to grow smaller. Weiss slowed until the car caught up.

"It is," Weiss said, "like fishing. You must play them just so."

"Now I understand," Benjy said. "You are trying to teach us how to fish."

All three laughed.

Again Weiss picked up speed.

Again the car behind them started to lose ground.

"Where did you get this automobile?" Itchy said.

"It is one of a kind," Weiss said.

"Too bad," Itchy said.

"If it has babies," Benjy said, "save one for me."

All three laughed.

The detective turned onto a side road, pulled to a stop, and doused the headlights. Presently the black touring car sped by.

"There they go," Itchy said.

"And good riddance," Weiss said. "When we return to the plant, these hard cases will still be beating the bushes for us out here. By the time they get back, we will be long gone."

Weiss pulled a gold watch out of his vest pocket, and glanced at it.

He nodded in satisfaction.

"It is almost time," he said.

"I'm glad to hear that," Itchy said. "But what are you talking about?"

"For you gentlemen to meet a friend of mine," Weiss said.

"It's always a pleasure to meet friends of yours," Itchy said.

"Thank you," Weiss said.

"What," Itchy said, "is he doing out here?"

"I sent for him," Weiss said.

"What does he do?" Benjy said.

"He breaks into things," Weiss said.

"What kind of things?" Itchy said.

"Anything and everything," Weiss said.

"That sounds very good," Itchy said.

"It is better than that," Weiss said. "It is outstanding."

Thirty-two

If there were a Yiddish army in New York, I would be one of its generals. It is not a bad idea, but obviously not as much fun as being a private detective and your own boss.

FROM THE CASEBOOKS OF MORRIS WEISS

Weiss cruised through the darkness, up the snow-covered dirt road, then turned back toward the plant. On the approach, he turned his headlights off. Itchy and Benjy both had their guns out and were peering out the back window. But not very anxiously.

"Nothing in back," Itchy said.

All three were silent for a moment.

"So tell me," Benjy said, "why are we here again?"

"You know," Itchy said, "I was starting to wonder the same thing."

Weiss grinned.

"You will soon see for yourselves," he said.

"I can hardly wait," Itchy said.

"Being with you, Morry," Benjy said, "is always an experience."

"And sometimes," Itchy said, "even a good one."

"I will use you as a reference," the detective said.

All the plant windows were dark when they reached the building. Weiss parked in back. They waited only a few seconds before they heard a tapping on the right front window. Weiss leaned across the empty seat and opened the car door. Cold air blew in.

"Make it snappy," Weiss said grinning, delighted with the phrase.

A small, thirtyish man climbed in and seated himself next to the detective.

He wore a black-belted trench coat and black felt hat. The coat was buttoned up to his neck. He had on black galoshes and black leather gloves. A black muffler rounded out the combination.

"You think wearing black makes you invisible, Mayer?" Weiss said.

"Only a little bit, Morris. But you know what they say?"

"Every little bit helps?"

"How did you know?"

"I heard you say it often enough," Weiss said.

Both men smiled.

The detective handled the introductions. First he told Mayer Greenberg about his two friends.

Greenberg said, "I know your bakery."

"How do you like it?" Benjy said.

"He is fishing for a compliment," Weiss told Greenberg.

"He deserves one," Greenberg said. "I would go miles for your cupcakes. Or at least down to the corner."

"See?" Benjy said.

"I must like the bakery a lot," Greenberg said patting his perfectly flat abdomen, "because I shop there so often."

"He has told me in the strictest confidence," Weiss said, "that it reminds him of the old country."

"Really?" Benjy said.

"He has no higher praise," Weiss said grinning.

Greenberg nodded happily.

Then Weiss told his two friends about Greenberg.

"Mayer Greenberg," he said, "fought with the partisans in the Vilna woods in Poland. We met near the end of the war. The Allies needed as much information about German troop movements as they could get. The partisans had used his extraordinary talents as a burglar to get items they needed for their fight. Because we both spoke Yiddish, I was given the job of interviewing him. I did the job so well we are still talking."

"So what is your line of work now?" Benjy said.

Greenberg shrugged.

"Before the war I was only a small-time burglar," Greenberg said.

"And now?" Itchy said

"A not-so-small-time burglar," Greenberg said.

"A big-time burglar?" Itchy said.

Greenberg shrugged.

"When the need arises," he said.

"This is progress," Itchy said.

"And you are here now . . . ?" Benjy said.

"To give you a demonstration," Greenberg said wiggling his gloved fingers.

"That is very kind of you," Itchy said, "considering we have never met before."

"And, of course, to help my good friend Morris," Greenberg said, "who invited me."

"Ah-ha," Itchy said.

"Thank you for coming, Mayer," Weiss said.

"It is always a pleasure to lend you a hand," Greenberg said. "In fact, while I was waiting, I took some first steps. If you will follow me. . . ."

Everyone piled out of the car.

Greenberg marched over to the back door of the plant, turned the knob, opened the door, and bowed.

"You make it look easy," Benjy said.

"It is easy, if you know how," Greenberg said holding the door open for the others.

They entered the building together in a good mood.

The gray concrete walls were waiting for them. In the night, they seemed especially frigid to Weiss.

What a hateful place, he thought, as the good mood dissipated.

"Which way?" Itchy said.

"Follow me," Weiss said, with more confidence than he felt.

He turned left.

The group stopped in front of Lazio's office.

Weiss tried the door. Locked. *Naturally. It is that kind of night.* He nodded to Greenberg, who produced a lock pick from his coat pocket and stepped over to the door.

Immediately Weiss heard a satisfying click.

"What did I tell you?" he said to his two friends. "He is the Heifetz of burglars."

"Maybe the Menuhin of burglars," Greenberg said. "Let us not exaggerate too much, or it may come back to haunt us."

Itchy shrugged.

"What does it matter?" he said. "Menuhin and Heifetz are both great artists."

"True enough," Weiss said.

He pushed open the door. And stepped into the office.

Bill Lazio was lying stretched out on the floor in a pool of his own blood. The small safe was where Weiss had last seen it. But now its door hung open. Empty.

The detective sighed.

He kneeled down and felt for the foreman's pulse. There was none.

"Well, gentlemen," he said, "what do you think?"

"I think," Greenberg said, backing away, "I am too young to go to jail."

"We are all too young," Benjy said.

"We must leave this place at once," Greenberg said.

But Weiss was already leading them out. He sprinted down the concrete hallway to the outside. He could hear a distant siren growing closer. He hoped to be far away by the time it reached the plant.

Thirty-three

The Yiddish word for thief is gonif. This is such a power-ful word, it has seeped into many languages. Still, nothing beats givald, which means help. Especially when encountering a gonif.

FROM THE CASEBOOKS OF MORRIS WEISS

It was midnight by the time Weiss let himself into Ida's flat on East Fifty-second. She was still up, as he knew she would be, seated on the new yellow living room sofa, engrossed in what he was sure was a very good book.

This was his home away from home, his refuge from being a detective, and all that entailed, which was plenty. And an exceedingly fine refuge it was, too. Because it contained his sweetheart, Ida.

Music came from the floor-model phonograph. He recognized Beethoven's Fifth Symphony. It sounded to Weiss like the Toscanini record. *It is not for nothing I am a detective*, he thought happily.

Ida put down the book she was reading.

"Moisheleh," she said.

"In person," he said grinning at her. "Accept no substitutes."

"Never," she said. And laughed.

"Fortunately, we see eye to eye on this," Weiss said.

The couple embraced.

Then Weiss followed her into the kitchen where she poured him a glass of tea—two teaspoons of sugar and a slice of lemon. Then, arm in arm, they returned to the living room and seated themselves on the large overstuffed sofa.

"So tell me," Ida said, "what is going on?"

The detective shrugged.

"So far, Idaleh, I am still looking for Lefkowitz."

"You are at least coming close?"

"I always come close. Only sometimes not close enough."

"And this is one of those times, Moisheleh?"

"Not if I can help it," he said. "What I have found out is that Jake Lefkowitz is not the man I thought he was. First of all, despite being married, he has a girlfriend on the side. A blond *shiksa* no less. This is a complication I never expected."

"What does it mean?"

Weiss shrugged.

"Who knows? Probably nothing," he said. "Worse yet, there are gangsters involved in all this. The boss is sitting in jail, and the underlings, including his family, are fighting it out between themselves for control of the outfit."

"Moisheleh, it sounds very complicated."

"You're telling me?"

Thirty-four

Most people rarely ask for trouble. Private detectives are the exception to this rule. They must ask. It's how they make their living.

FROM THE CASEBOOKS OF MORRIS WEISS

"A great good morning to you, Mr. Weiss."

"And the same to you, Sergeant O'Toole."

Weiss had walked into his friend's office carrying two containers of coffee and six donuts in a brown paper bag, as was his habit when visiting the sergeant. He hung his coat on the back of a black folding chair, seated himself comfortably, and pushed the paper bag across O'Toole's desk.

"Help yourself, Sergeant," he said. "Straight from Fishman's Bakery, and right from the oven."

"Ah," O'Toole said with a delighted grin on his face, as if he'd just won the Irish Sweepstakes. Although in truth, Weiss always brought coffee and donuts and always from the Orchard Street Bakery.

"You know the way to a man's heart, Mr. Weiss."

"I know the way to *your* heart, Sergeant O'Toole. Through *your* stomach."

O'Toole nodded.

"I am delighted to tell you, Mr. Weiss," he said, "that is indeed the right direction."

Both men laughed.

"You are here early today," the sergeant said.

The detective took a swallow of coffee and a bite of a cake donut with powdered sugar on top.

"Not early," he said. "Late."

Weiss took another swallow.

The bakery's coffee gets better each week, he thought. *One of the many bonuses, no doubt, of coming here to visit my old friend. Or, I could brew the coffee at home. But then I would be missing the donuts.*

Weiss said, "I never even made it home last night."

The sergeant leaned back in his chair.

"A criminal investigation?"

Weiss grinned.

"Something much better," he said.

"Ah, your lady friend, is it?"

"It is."

"I met her," the sergeant said. "A wonderful woman."

"Thank you," Weiss said. "She likes you, too."

"You two make a fine couple."

Weiss smiled.

"I think so myself," he said.

Weiss helped himself to another donut, this time one without sugar.

"Planning to tie the knot, Mr. Weiss?"

"The thought has occurred to me," Weiss said.

"So what are you waiting for? You won't be young forever."

The detective shrugged.

"She," he said, "usually goes on long tours with her quartet. And I, of course, have criminals to keep me busy a lot of the time. I worry about that."

"Who wouldn't? Still, you couldn't find a better girl. And marriage is a glorious institution."

Weiss nodded.

"I know it," he said.

By then they had both finished off the donuts and the two containers of coffee.

Weiss smiled.

"Thank you for the encouragement," he said.

O'Toole said, "You would do the same for me, Mr. Weiss."

"You can count on it," Weiss said. "Has anything happened to come over the wire about Hunts Point this morning?"

"Hunts Point? Let me check."

The sergeant rose to go, looked down, and scooped up a gray cat. "To keep you company while I am gone," he said.

And plunked the cat down on Weiss's lap.

"The precinct mascot," O'Toole said.

Detective and cat stared at each other.

Weiss scratched the cat behind the left ear.

The cat said, *"Meow."*

"It has a name?" Weiss said.

"Twobits," the sergeant said, and left.

"You are worth more than two bits, aren't you?" Weiss said. But the cat merely looked at him and remained noncommittal.

Presently the sergeant returned and Twobits departed.

"Well," the sergeant said, "you must have been on to something. The lads found a body."

"In the meatpacking plant?"

"Near it," O'Toole said. "Buried under a mound of snow."

"The foreman, Lazio, eh?"

"At this point, Mr. Weiss, that is anyone's guess."

"His wallet was gone?"

The sergeant nodded.

"How was he killed?"

"Shot in the head, point-bank."

"Sounds like an execution."

"So it does."

Thirty-five

The trouble with being a private detective on the Lower East Side is that some of your clients won't have enough money to pay your fee. Don't worry. You can always work out an installment plan with them. If they vanish before it is all paid back, you can track them down. After all, you are a private detective.

FROM THE CASEBOOKS OF MORRIS WEISS

"Thank you for the company" Weiss said. **"It is** very welcome."

"I wouldn't have you going to this place alone, Mr. Weiss."

"Really?"

The sergeant nodded.

"After all these years," he said, "it still turns my stomach."

"My feelings exactly," Weiss said.

The two friends were in the city mortuary, the cadavers on either side of them stacked on metal slabs, one on top of the other. The smell of death seemed to hang in the air. Fortunately, they were behind closed drawers. Outside the temperature was in the

136

low twenties, but to Weiss it seemed colder in the mortuary.

The detective sighed.

"I used to think," he said, "that someday all these cadavers would jump out and start dancing around me."

"Merely a touch of dementia," the sergeant said. "Nothing to worry about."

"Now you tell me," Weiss said.

Both men laughed uproariously.

Even the attendant who was guiding them broke into a broad grin.

O'Toole shook his head.

"It is a bit more than dementia, however," he said. "It is full-blown lunacy."

"That is what I was afraid of," the detective said. "Full-blown is the worst kind."

This time it was the attendant who began laughing first.

"We should play the Palace, Mr. Weiss. Our fortunes will be made."

"Only if he's in the audience," Weiss said pointing to the attendant.

The attendant smiled.

"We're here, gents," he said.

"Ah," the sergeant said.

"If that was a sigh of relief," Weiss said, "then I wholeheartedly agree."

The attendant opened the drawer.

"Take a gander," he said.

The two friends stepped up to the slab and looked down. A short, corpulent man lay there. But it was not Frank Lazio, the plant foreman. The slab was taken up by the last remains of Laib Domb, the bookie.

Thirty-six

Being a private detective allows you to meet many people you would otherwise not meet. Nor ever want to. Be assured, the feeling will be mutual.

FROM THE CASEBOOKS OF MORRIS WEISS

Just as Laib Domb was corpulent, so the man who now took his place was skinny. He wore a green striped shirt under a blue blazer, along with bright red suspenders. On the street, they would call a man who wore such an outfit a "sport." The detective, from where he stood, could not see his shoes, but was willing to bet they were white.

This fellow, Weiss thought, *is obviously a refugee from a Li'l Abner comic strip. But no one's let him in on the secret yet.*

"Who sent you here?" the man said.

"I sent myself," Weiss said.

The man, who had given his name as Moisha Pupik, a gag name which meant Moisha Bellybutton, said, "Then why should I tell you anything, mister?"

139

Weiss said, "It will make things easier for you."

Pupik waved a hand.

"Let them be hard," he said.

"Who gave you this job?" Weiss said.

"I looked in the help wanted section of *Der Tog*."

Weiss shook his finger at the man.

"Don't say I didn't warn you," he said.

Pupik shrugged.

"I'll say what I want, mister. It's a free country."

Weiss, feigning anger, turned on his heel and stormed from the office. He did not stop to chat with some of the familiar faces in the gambling room. But instead ran out the door at full tilt, down the stairs, and onto the street. He did not have far to go, only a few feet to the right, and through the conveniently unlocked door of Fishman's Bakery. He hurried by the hot ovens without pausing, as he usually did, to inhale the aroma of what was baking there, and down the wooden stairs that ended in the basement. Marvin Lowenstein, from the District Attorney's office, removed a pair of earphones, and greeted him with a wave of his hand.

Lowenstein was a dapper man in his mid thirties. He had graduated from Columbia University and had fully expected to enter an upscale law firm when the Great Depression tripped him up. He settled for the D.A.'s office and there he remained. Weiss liked him.

"You've missed nothing yet," he said.

"So what's happening?" Weiss said.

"Dead air," Lowenstein said.

"Tell me," the detective said, "why do you do this kind of work yourself? Doesn't your office have specialists?"

"Sure. But this isn't for my office."

"Who is the beneficiary of your expertise?"

"Us mostly."

"How nice for us," Weiss said.

"It lets me keep my hand in."

Weiss sat down on a kitchen chair and was given a pair of earphones. He heard nothing. Then a woman's voice said, "He bothers no one."

"He bothers me, lady."

"Why? What has he done to you?"

"Nothin' yet."

"So?"

"A lotta our guys are sittin' in stir 'cause of him."

"Because they are stupid."

"I don't wanna be one of 'em, lady."

"Do not worry, you won't be."

"Easy for you to say."

"Why?"

"You ain't out on the firing line."

"I told you not to worry."

"Sure, sure. You told me."

And they both hung up.

Weiss and Lowenstein sat in the silence and looked at each other.

"Make anything of that?" Lowenstein said.

Weiss nodded.

"Unfortunately," he said.

"So, don't keep me in suspense."

"That was the man who now runs the gambling operation upstairs," Weiss said. "He's the one who told me his name is Moisha Pupik."

"A comedian, ah?"

"A side-splitter," Weiss said.

"And the woman?"

The detective sighed.

"She is Fraydela Gold," he said.

"You don't sound happy," Lowenstein said.

Weiss shrugged.

"I'm not," he said.

"What has she done?"

"I think she had me fooled," Weiss said, "by pretending to be one of us. Instead, she is one of them."

"Really?"

"Absolutely," Weiss said. "But if you tell anyone, I will deny it."

Lowenstein chuckled.

"I hate being fooled," the detective said.

Lowenstein began putting away his equipment.

"Who doesn't?" he said. "If nothing else, it's bad for business."

"That woman," Weiss said, "she may actually run this Pupik fellow. And probably Albert, Leo, and Joey, too."

"Her sons, eh?"

"So it seems."

Weiss and Lowenstein headed for the stairs.

"Thank you for the help," Weiss said.

"Anytime," Lowenstein said. "Within reason, of course."

"Of course."

Thirty-seven

*The Lower East Side someday will lose its Yiddish-
speaking population. The bakeries, of course, will be the
last to go. My wife Ida is such a great cook and baker that
I will no doubt manage to survive without them. But
what will other people do?*

FROM THE CASEBOOKS OF MORRIS WEISS

"It is up there," Weiss said, **"on the second floor.**
To the left of the bakery."

"They gamble there?" Boris Minsky said.

"At night and into the early morning."

"And then they go to work?"

"Oh, yes," Weiss said. "Or they try to."

"It is not a pretty business," Minsky said, "is it?"

"No," Weiss said. "Unless they are big winners.
That, of course, changes everything."

"Of course," Minsky said.

The two men stood on the street across from the
gambling hall, looking up at the second floor. A cold
wind was blowing over the snow-covered streets.
Both wore gloves and mufflers. But only Minsky
wore galoshes.

144

"I have," Minsky said, "only one more question."

"By all means," the detective said.

"What are we doing here?"

"Showing our colors," Weiss said.

"I beg your pardon?"

"Letting them know we are here."

"I thought we wished to do just the opposite."

"Usually."

"But not now?"

"Quite right," the detective said. "Now we want only to draw their attention to our presence."

"Why?"

"It will give them food for thought."

"Your concern for their mental faculties does you credit."

"Thank you, Boris. Also, it may prompt them to some kind of rash action."

"Yes," Minsky said. "They may try to shoot me."

"Not that rash."

"I trust they are aware of that."

"In any case," Weiss said, "you will not be alone."

"I will not?"

"Hardly."

"That is a comfort."

"Come," Weiss said. "Let us cross over to the bakery. It is time for a break."

The two men crossed the street and entered the bakery.

The detective handled the introductions, then he

and Minsky went behind the counter and back past the ovens.

A small group met them downstairs in the basement, all eating slices of cake and pie.

Weiss waved a greeting.

"This is my associate, Boris Minsky," he said.

Minsky nodded.

"This looks like a detective's convention," he said.

"Or a group of bakery addicts," Benjy said. "Maybe we should start a club?"

"We will call it the Very Big *Fresers*," Itchy said.

"Seems appropriate," Weiss said. To Minsky he said, "It means 'very big gobblers.'"

Itchy offered Weiss and Minsky each a slice of peach pie.

"There's apple, too," he said.

Weiss grinned, thanked him, and ate it before someone could take it away from him. Minsky looked at his, sniffed it delicately, and then took a large bite.

"Excellent," he said.

"Of course," Benjy said.

"It pays to come to the right place," the detective said.

"Only in this case," Benjy said, "there are two right places, ours and their's. Fishman's and the Orchard Street Bakery, where Itchy and I both work and have a piece of the action. These two places are the unofficial extension of the Weiss office."

"And this means what?" Minsky said.

"Plenty of good, free food," Itchy said.

"And sometimes even free help," Benjy said.

"It is true," Weiss said. "Their generosity is outstanding. Right, gentlemen?"

"We are a bargain," Benjy said, "any way you look at it."

"Also," Weiss said, "this is an inspiring atmosphere."

By now Itchy had spliced together the wires of his two-reel recorder with those of the phone company.

Benjy had donned a pair of earphones.

"Well?" the detective said.

"Nothing doing," said Itchy.

"Obviously," Weiss said, "they need more inspiration."

"Does that mean going back into the cold?" Minsky said.

"Only for a short while, Boris."

"Even that will be too long," Minsky said.

"We will have to create some activity to attract their attention," Weiss said.

"That," Minsky said, "sounds hard."

"Not when done by an expert," Weiss said and smiled.

Thirty-eight

If you want to be married and a private detective, it is important to find a wife who, if nothing else, can put up with the crazy hours you may have to work. I have found such a wife. Of course, I am, after all, a private detective, and finding people is one of my specialties.

FROM THE CASEBOOKS OF MORRIS WEISS

It had grown dark.

Weiss and Minsky paced under the recently lit street lamps across from the gambling hall. Every few seconds one or the other would point up toward the second-floor windows. They appeared to be engaged in a heated discussion.

Minsky said, "I feel like a fool."

Weiss said, "Not to the ones who think they are being watched."

"I have seen no watchers."

"Trust me, Boris, they are us."

"Us?"

"Of course. And to them *we* is serious business."

"If you say so," Minsky said.

"I do. They will think we are arguing about *them*."

"So?"

"It will make them uncomfortable."

"It is making *me* uncomfortable," Minsky said.

"But not as uncomfortable as our friends up there, eh?"

"I see," Minsky said.

Weiss smiled.

"Remember," he said, "they have paid off the local authorities, or they would not be staying here at all. They will now wonder if they have gotten their money's worth."

"And we will do what?" Minsky said.

"Let them wonder," Weiss said.

Thirty-nine

*As a child, I sang in a Yiddish youth chorus. I still re-
member some of the songs. They were easier to do than
Beethoven, and at the time seemed equally rewarding. Of
course, I was very young then.*

FROM THE CASEBOOKS OF MORRIS WEISS

"Listen to this," Itchy said, and clicked on a
switch.

The two-reel tape recorder began to whir.

A deep male voice said, "What the hell's goin' on
with you guys?"

"We got a problem," a hoarse voice answered.

Weiss thought, *Ah, a three-pack smoker.*

"Some guy bustin' t'bank?"

"Not that kinda problem."

What, a stickup?"

"Uh-uh."

The deep voice sighed.

"Okay, let's hear it. I bet it's a beaut."

Itchy laughed.

"He'd win that bet, too," Benjy said.

150

"There's a coupla guys downstairs on the street."

"On the street?"

"They keep pointin' up here," the hoarse voice whined.

"So what's it to you?"

"They're makin' me nervous."

"Take a drink."

"Ain't gonna help."

"It better. I ain't got time for this crap."

Forty

Who knows? Maybe I could have been a champion boxer like Benny Leonard. In the long run, of course, it is no way to maintain your health. I might have been a classical musician but, alas, I lacked the talent. Instead, I became a private detective. I could tell you how successful I am, but it is better to let my deeds speak for me. Who is going to hire an egotistical private detective?

FROM THE CASEBOOKS OF MORRIS WEISS

The sun shone down on Weiss. But it was still cold. *Maybe I'll have another cup of coffee, after all*, he thought. *I survived the last cup in this place, why not this one? I know Jake is certainly not hiding in this candy store. Nor does it seem that old man Kressky has information about my missing printer. Yet you can never tell. Something may turn up.*

He pushed open the door, briefcase in hand.

He smelled coffee, all right. But even stronger was the overwhelming odor of cigarette smoke.

A good thing children don't come in here very often, he thought. *It would undermine their health. Just inhaling the air in here is undermining mine.*

"Good morning, Kressky," he said.

Neither the old man behind the counter nor the

candy store around him had changed since his last visit, which was, after all, only a few days ago. There were still no newspapers, magazines, or even more comic books. Candy itself was in very short supply. But that was not the store's main purpose, as Weiss knew. The gambling hall was directly above the store. Kressky was the lookout.

"How are you, Morry?" Kressky said.

"Excellent," Weiss said.

"What can I get you?"

"Coffee, maybe," Weiss said, seating himself at the counter.

"Maybe? You are not sure?"

Weiss smiled.

"How long has that coffee been sitting there?"

Kressky shrugged.

"A day or two," he said.

"Has it killed any customers yet?" the detective said in Yiddish.

"Who knows? They do not stay long enough to die on the spot. If they die, it happens on the street." Kressky laughed. His laugh ended in a racking cough. Snatching a crumpled hanky from his pants pocket, he spit into it, folded it carefully, and returned it to his pocket.

Weiss decided to forgo the coffee.

"Kressky," he said, "I want you to listen to something."

"What?"

"You will hear."

Weiss opened his briefcase and took out the two-reel tape recorder and a small speaker and put them on the counter.

"Very fancy," the storekeeper said.

"Where is the outlet?" Weiss said.

"Back here," Kressky said. "Where else should it be?"

"Very good. Plug it in, please."

The storekeeper did as instructed.

"You should also lock the door," Weiss said.

Kressky shrugged.

"Who comes in here?" he said.

"Lock it anyway."

"If you say so."

Kressky shuffled to the end of the counter, walked around it, and locked the door. He slowly returned to his former position behind the counter.

"Satisfied?" he asked.

Weiss gave a short bow and flicked a switch on the tape recorder.

The phone conversation that Itchy and Benjy had recorded came over the speaker. Weiss recognized the voice of the man who told him he was Moisha Pupik.

"Who is the one with the deep voice?" the detective asked.

Kressky stared at the recorder in wonder. And shrugged. "It sounds like Yankel Gold's son Joey."

"From them you take your orders?" Weiss said.

"What orders?" Kressky said. "You know what I do here, Morry. I sit and watch out that everything is all right. If something, God forbid, looks wrong, I press a button behind the counter and the boys from upstairs come right down."

Weiss nodded.

"So who is Moisha Pupik?"

"He is Manny Zilberfarb. Only to you is he Moisha Pupik."

"And he is your boss, eh?"

Kressky shrugged, getting suddenly busy wiping the counter.

"These days he pays me my money. But he is not the real boss. The real one is Yankel Gold, but he is these days sitting in prison again. It's in and out, then in again for that man. Don't say I told you anything. I don't want to get in trouble. You understand?"

Weiss nodded.

"And no one has said a word about Jake?" he said.

"No one. As though he has fallen off the face of the earth."

"That is all you have to tell me, Kressky?"

"That is all," Kressky shrugged. "But what do I know?"

"Enough," Weiss said.

Forty-one

My nephew Max is a natural private detective. Four years of college didn't diminish his abilities at all. And when he needed special guidance, there was always the one-man college of Morris Weiss to help him. Now that's a college I can recommend without reservation.

FROM THE CASEBOOKS OF MORRIS WEISS

Weiss knocked on the door.

"Yes? Who is it?"

"Morris Weiss, the detective."

"How nice," the voice of Fraydela Gold said.

The door opened at once.

"Mrs. Gold," Weiss said, extending his hand. "It is a great pleasure to see you again."

"It is *my* pleasure," she said, and ushered Weiss into the living room.

He put his briefcase on the floor.

He placed his coat, hat, and muffler on the couch and then seated himself comfortably next to them.

"Wait here," she said.

She will return with a plate of cookies and a glass of tea. Not for nothing am I a detective.

The cookies turned out to be egg cookies just like the last time. The tea was in a tall glass. There were slices of lemon in one dish and cubes of sugar in another. Weiss had no complaints.

"Thank you," he said.

"Now," she said, "what can I do for you, dear Mr. Weiss?"

The detective reached down for his briefcase and opened it.

"I want you to hear something," he said.

"I would be delighted."

He took out the tape recorder.

"Where can I plug this in?" Weiss said.

"Behind the couch. Here."

She showed him where.

"Very good," he said, flicking the switch on the recorder.

The spools began to turn, voices began to talk.

"Recognize anyone?" he said.

She put her hand to her mouth.

"It is my Joey," she said.

"Exactly," Weiss said. "His deep voice is outstanding."

"How did you come by this, Mr. Weiss?"

The tape had run its course. The detective turned it off and smiled at his hostess.

"It is a copy I took from the police," he said.

"They gave it to you?"

"I didn't steal it," he said honestly enough.

"I don't understand. You are a policeman?"

"Hardly. But I often work with them. We help each other out. But when I heard this at the station, I asked for a copy."

"I still do not understand, Mr. Weiss."

The detective smiled.

"It is simple," he said. "I enjoyed myself so much here last time that I wanted to find some way to show my appreciation. This is it. I am sure you will do the right thing, eh? You will let Joey know?"

"Definitely."

"Excellent," he said taking her hand and bowing over it. Then, gloves, muffler, and hat in hand, with trench coat slung over his arm, he all but flew from the apartment.

Forty-two

On the Lower East Side, you didn't have gyms to join to stay in shape. Just climbing all those tenement stairs was like belonging to five gyms.

From the casebooks of Morris Weiss

Once down the stairs, Weiss looked up.

Nothing seemed even remotely out of place, except maybe the two repairmen working on the telephone lines up above. They were laughing. Weiss nodded almost imperceptibly. And continued on his way toward the next block. Behind him, the two repairmen began to climb down.

The three assembled out of sight of Mrs. Gold's building.

"Well?" Weiss said.

"I don't think you have quite won her over," Itchy said.

"What makes you say that?" Weiss said.

"This Joey is her son?" Benjy said.

"He has a deep voice?" the detective said.

159

"Like an opera singer." Benjy said. "Only talking."

"That's the boy," Weiss said. "Anyway, at least I think so."

"She phoned him right after you left."

"And," Itchy said, "he was all for gunning you down like the mad dog you are."

"But she wouldn't let him," Benjy said.

"What did I tell you?" Weiss said.

"No," Itchy said. "She wanted them to first make sure you really deserved it."

Weiss said, "Deserved it? This is your idea of a joke, eh?"

"Some joke," Itchy said. "We can do better than that without really trying."

"Well," the detective said, "I will go have another talk with her."

"And what will that do?"

"Convince her that I don't deserve to be murdered."

Forty-three

———

*There are no uncle-and-nephew private detective teams
in literature as far as I know. And unless some smart
young fellow writes a book about us, so it will remain.*

FROM THE CASEBOOKS OF MORRIS WEISS

The detective knocked on the door. It opened almost
immediately.

"Please come in," a beaming Mrs. Gold said.

Returning her smile, Morris Weiss entered the
flat.

"Mrs. Gold," he said. "It is very good to see you
again."

"I knew you would be back, Mr. Weiss," she said.
"Just not so soon."

"Then you are a better detective than I am," he
said smiling.

"Why is that?"

"I had absolutely no idea I was going to do such a
thing until a moment ago."

"When my boy called for your—"

"Untimely demise?" Weiss said.

"Yes," she said. "So you *were* listening in!"

Weiss shrugged.

"That is how I earn my keep," he said.

"I will not hold it against you," Mrs. Gold said.

"Thank you," Weiss said. "That is nice of you."

"Let me assure you, dear Mr. Weiss, it was only a test."

Weiss raised an eyebrow.

"Like in public school?" he said.

"More advanced," she said, giggling into her hand like the schoolgirl she wasn't. "But where are my manners. Please, come and sit."

She's crazy. Now it becomes obvious, he thought as he followed her into the familiar room. Again, he carefully folded his coat on the back of a chair, and placed his hat on top of it. He waited until she was seated, then sat next to her on the sofa.

"I passed, eh?"

"Oh, yes."

"That's nice," he said.

"With flying colors, as they say."

"They do say that, don't they? So tell me about this test?" he said. "You have completely aroused my interest."

"It was just a whim. I wondered if you trusted me, or were somehow listening in."

"Ah-ha. So you said something outrageous."

"Forgive me, Mr. Weiss, I did."

"But who wouldn't trust you?" Weiss said.

"Anyone who knows my husband."

"Really?"

"They would say it runs in the family," she said as a practiced tear ran down her cheek.

"It?"

"Crime, Mr. Weiss: hooliganism, depravity, dishonesty."

"I would never say anything like that about you, Mrs. Gold."

At least not within your hearing, he thought.

"I know you wouldn't," Mrs. Gold said. "From the first moment I saw you, I knew you were different."

"Thank you," the detective said.

And thought, *She is beginning to embarrass me.*

"Come," she said. "I want to show you something."

Weiss rose and followed her into the kitchen.

"This," she said, "is my dumbwaiter."

The detective looked at the small door in the wall next to the oven and nodded. *Am I supposed to compliment her on that? When they are crazy, they are crazy.*

"I want you to meet someone," she said.

"My pleasure."

Mrs. Gold strode to the dumbwaiter and opened the door.

Must be someone very small, he thought, *if he's in there.* And tried hard to keep from laughing. *This case is getting the better of me.*

163

His hostess stuck her head into the shaft and yelled:

"Albert! Come up here."

"On my way, Ma!"

Forty-four

Having money is not everything. But there are times it might very well look like everything. Pay no attention to such times. They will only land you in the soup.

FROM THE CASEBOOKS OF MORRIS WEISS

Mrs. Gold turned to her guest.

"My middle son," she said.

"He lives here, eh?"

"Right below me," she said. "In these times, a mother needs her children close by. Don't you think so, Mr. Weiss?"

"Absolutely," he said.

What am I saying? he thought. *I don't even know what she's talking about.*

Presently, a tall, thirtyish man came through a doorway in the hall and into the living room. He wore gray pants and a white shirt. His sleeves were rolled up as if he was getting ready to work.

The detective rose from the sofa and the two men shook hands.

"Albert," she said, "this is Mr. Morris Weiss."

"The detective?"

"Yes," she said.

"You here to pinch my ma?" Albert said smiling.

"God forbid," Weiss said, also smiling. "I am a great admirer of your mother."

"Me, too," Albert said. "How can I help you?"

"Tell Mr. Weiss what is happening in the business," his mother said.

"*Our* business?"

"Of course," she said. "Who else's?"

Albert turned to the detective.

"Well, that's a new one," he said. "Usually, she warns me *not* to tell anyone."

"Go ahead, Albert," Mrs. Gold said. "It's all right."

"It's a bloody war!" Albert said with obvious delight. "With the boys from Laib Domb's and Bill Lazio's camp fighting it out."

Weiss sighed.

It's always nicer, he thought, *when other people are fighting the wars.*

"Why are they doing that?" Weiss said.

"Doing what?"

"Fighting each other?" Weiss said.

"Sit down, gentlemen, please," Mrs. Gold said.

Ever obedient, they sat.

"You've heard of Laib Domb, the bookie, I bet?" Albert said.

"You would win that bet," Weiss said.

"Well, with dad still in the hoosegow, the guys in the outfit began squabbling over the take."

"Whose side was Domb on?" Weiss said.

"His own. When dad was around to keep an eye on him, he behaved. But with dad on ice, it was another story. Now his second in command has taken over."

"Manny Zilberfarb," Weiss said.

Albert said, "You seem to know everything."

"Almost everything."

"Well, not everyone is ready to go along with Zilberfarb running the works."

"Ah-ha. And how does this sit with your husband?" She shrugged.

"Who knows?" Mrs. Gold said. "I see him once a month at the prison. And even then he doesn't always talk business with me. Why should he? He does well enough on his own."

"Ma loves to give out free advice," the son said.

"And sometimes she's even right, eh?" the detective said.

"Usually," Albert said.

"My son is my greatest admirer."

And she put an arm around his shoulder.

"What about Joey?" Weiss said.

"He is his father's son," Mrs. Gold said.

"Sides with the old man," Albert said.

"But we are still a family," Mrs. Gold said.

"We used to sit down at the same table at least once a year," Albert said, "before Dad landed in the clink."

They might as well be divorced, the detective thought.

"Sometimes even twice," Mrs. Gold said.

"I'm impressed," Weiss said.

"That was the idea," Albert said.

Everyone laughed.

Weiss said, "Have you heard anything about what happened to Bernard Loft?"

"Bernie? You working on that one?" the son said.

Weiss nodded.

He looked from mother to son. Neither spoke.

I've stopped them cold, he thought. *I hardly know my own power, it seems.*

"Tell him," Mrs. Gold finally said.

Albert shrugged.

"Sure," he said. "Why not? It's no skin off my nose."

Mrs. Gold stood, as if better to view the conversation.

"Listen," Albert said. "I think my old man began rocking the boat. Even from prison."

"Gold the Butcher?" Weiss said, because he liked the way it sounded.

"Yeah. That's what's going on, see?"

"Maybe," Weiss said, "I would see more if you gave me a few more details."

"Sure. My old man figured he still had control of the rackets while he was in stir. But he figured wrong."

"Albert, don't talk like that," his mother said. "You sound like a hoodlum."

"Sorry, Ma. Anyway, the guy who was second in command pushed out a lotta Pa's guys. Maybe Laib Domb did some pushing himself. They chose up sides like a football team and all hell began to break loose."

Too bad, Weiss thought, *no one is paying me for the lowdown on the Golds. About the Golds I now know. Can the inside track on Lefkowitz be far behind? Probably. A connection between Jake and the Golds is obviously the gambling rackets. But now that I know this, what do I know? It is still muddled. So where is Jake?*

"And now that your father is still behind bars?" the detective continued.

"Well, it's not every man for himself, but it's getting there. Pa will try to get back in control."

Weiss said, "What do you do for a living, Albert?"

"Me? I'm a freelance commercial artist."

"And a very good one," his mother said.

"Thanks, Ma," Albert said.

"I'm glad to hear that you have a worthwhile profession," Weiss said. "Where do you sell?"

"I've done a cover for *Dime Detective*, some illustrations for *Detective Fiction Weekly* and *Nickel*

Western, four jobs for *Spicy Detective*, and I almost made a sale to *Black Mask* last month."

"Hmm," Weiss said, not having heard of any of them.

"You ought to drop in sometime and take a look at my work," Albert said.

"It would be my pleasure," Morris Weiss said.

Forty-five

A few good friends in high places make an excellent bulwark against disaster. Unless, of course, they turn out to be crooks. If that happens, my best advice is: run for the hills.

FROM THE CASEBOOKS OF MORRIS WEISS

"Listen," Zilberfarb said, **"I don't care who you**
are, or how many friends you got. Hey, you listening?"

"Of course," Weiss said. "That is why I am here."

But the truth was he had caught Weiss glancing
through the half-open office door at the patrons in the
gambling hall, which he realized he had been neglecting. *Maybe*, he thought, *if I pay a bit more attention
to these gangster wars it will help me clean up the
gambling here and collect a nice check from this
Blottnick. That would be a very good piece of work.*

"Make trouble and out you go. Got that?" Zilberfarb said.

The detective shrugged.

"Who could fail to understand?" he said.

"Okay, just so you got that straight."

"I always heed good advice, Mr. Pupik—who wouldn't?"

"Look," Zilberfarb said, "we don't like wiseguys around here."

"You are," the detective said, "a hard man to please."

"Do me a favor. Go to one of the tables," Zilberfarb said, "and lose some money. Don't bother me."

Zilberfarb wore a striped black-and-white jacket, a blue-and-white-striped shirt, and a red-and-green polka-dot tie. Not for nothing was the translation of his name "silver paint."

Always the sport, Weiss thought. *I must be doing something wrong to keep bumping into such characters.*

Through the half-open door the detective could still hear the roar of voices. *If anything*, he thought, *they had grown even louder*. Small clouds of cigarette and cigar smoke rose toward the ceiling. The voices babbled incessantly, cursing, laughing, arguing. *This must be what an insane asylum is like at lunchtime*, the detective thought. *If they let all the inmates into the dining room at the same time.*

"I am not here to make trouble," Weiss said.

"Says you."

"I'm here to maybe save your life, Zilberfarb."

"Don't do me no favors, pal. I'll save my own life."

Weiss shrugged.

"If you are lucky," he said.

"Lucky is my middle name," Zilberfarb said.

"If Lady Luck walks out on you, my friend, you will be dead."

"All right. Enough! Let's hear it, already." Zilberfarb fell back into a worn overstuffed chair, folded his skinny arms across his chest, and cocked his head in an exaggerated "listening" pose.

"The word is out on the street," Weiss said. "A big loser here thinks he was cheated. He is telling people that you are the one who did it and that he will kill you. It is as simple as that."

Or as complicated, Weiss thought. *Who knows? Maybe this will result in some kind of movement.*

"Yeah? Tell me something new. We get dozens of 'em each year. People like to sound off. Why's this one so different?"

"The man has a gun," Weiss said.

"Lotsa guys got guns."

"Yes. But this man has a bullet earmarked for you, Mr. Zilberfarb. And he is boasting about it all over town."

"The guy got a name?"

"I am sure his parents did not neglect to give him one. Unfortunately, I do not know it."

"So tell me something. How come you're here giving me this big tip? We ain't exactly chummy, are we, Weiss?"

"I will tell you," the detective said. "In my business,

it doesn't pay to antagonize people needlessly. This information I'm giving you, Mr. Zilberfarb, for what it is worth, should straighten things out between us, eh?"

"We'll see what it's worth," Zilberfarb said. "Won't we, pal?"

Forty-six

They say it takes one to know one. If this were really true, all the private detectives would be crooks. Along with the police, FBI, and the Secret Service agents.

FROM THE CASEBOOKS OF MORRIS WEISS

Weiss moved fast. He ran from the premises at top speed, taking the stairs three at a time. *They will think I don't like this place, and they will be absolutely right.*

The street was already dark when he hit the sidewalk, and almost devoid of people. Fishman's Bakery was next door. Ordinarily the front door to the bakery would at this hour be locked. But it had thoughtfully been left unlocked for the detective. He stepped inside without hesitation, hurried by the empty glass cases and to the doorway behind the counter, then down a flight of stairs to the basement.

Lowenstein from the D.A.'s office was there in a blue jacket, a white starched shirt, and earphones. A two-reel tape recorder was whirring away.

Weiss waved a greeting.

"What have I missed?" he called out.

"Nothing yet," Lowenstein said.

"So what's going on?"

"Plenty of dead air. But all this will change very shortly."

"Yes?" Weiss said. "Why?"

"Your friend, Zilberfarb, from upstairs called his boss to ask what to do."

"He called Gold the Butcher?"

"That's the one."

"He's out of prison?"

"Not yet. But he seems to have special privileges. He's probably speaking from the warden's office on a secure line."

"And what did Gold have to say?"

"He's saying it now."

Lowenstein removed his earphones.

"Give a listen," he said, tossing them to the detective.

"I got my book out, boss," Zilberfarb was saying. "We'll find out in a jiffy."

"Make it snappy," Gold said.

"I'm goin' as fast as I can."

"This is commendable," Weiss said.

"What is commendable?" Lowenstein said, as though he doubted anything could be good in this lamentable situation.

He may be right, Weiss thought.

But what he said was, "They are doing my job for me."

"Really?" Lowenstein said.

"What could be better?" Weiss said.

"A different job, maybe?"

Weiss grinned and shook his head.

"The job is fine," he said. "It is in the details that problems arise."

"And what's happening now?"

"The Butcher is being read a list of names," Weiss said. "And the details may now be beginning to make problems for the other side."

"Lots of big losers."

"Plenty of them."

"Know any?"

"Personally, only one," Weiss said. "And he is once removed."

"What do you mean?" Lowenstein said.

"I have recently met a friend of the late Bernie Loft named Yossel Korn in Fishman's Bakery in the dead of night. Their list of big losers has an Abe Korn. This Abe could be Yossie's relative. A brother maybe or a father, or even a cousin."

"That is not much," Lowenstein said.

"True. But it's a start. And to reach the finish you must make a start, eh?"

"So, you're a philosopher, too."

"Only," Weiss said, "in my spare time."

"Want me to check out this Korn fellow?"

"It may not be necessary."

"Why's that?"

"He may be in the phone book."

"The phone book?"

"It is something we fellows who don't work for a salary try to do," Weiss said. "Find the shortest and easiest way to end a job."

Forty-seven

My nephew Max has a private detective for a girlfriend. This I like to call the double whammy. And if it doesn't work, there is always Uncle Morris to come to the rescue.

FROM THE CASEBOOKS OF MORRIS WEISS

Next morning Weiss walked to the office, seated himself at his desk, and tried the phone book. *The easy way first, eh?*

The thing to do, obviously, was call Yossie and ask if there was an Abe in his family.

Of course, there was no Yossel Korn listed. That would have been *too* easy. Yossel was a Yiddish name. Only extreme Yiddish patriots or professional Yiddishists would put that name in the phone book. Yossel was neither. He had identified himself as a carpenter.

Jack was English for Yossel.

The detective found more than one Jack Korn in the phone book. There were six of them in all who lived on the Lower East Side. The two who picked up were the wrong Jacks. The rest were not home. He tried the listing for *carpenter* in the yellow pages. There were plenty of those but no Jacks. *I am wasting my time*, Weiss thought.

He rose from behind his desk, stretched, and seated himself again. Inspiration had failed to appear.

When that happened to Weiss, there was only one thing to do: he called Sergeant O'Toole.

"Good morning, Sergeant," the detective said. "It's Weiss."

"And a grand good morning to you, Mr. Weiss."

"It's the Bernie Loft case."

"Ah," the sergeant said, "that one, is it? Well, rest assured, Mr. Weiss, I have checked, and this Loft is still dead."

Both men roared with laughter.

Weiss said, "That's very bad."

"True," the sergeant said. "It doesn't get any worse, especially for this Loft."

After the levity again subsided, Weiss said, "I am trying to find out what became of one Abe Korn."

"Well, Mr. Weiss, have you thought of hiring a private detective?"

They both laughed again.

"And have him show me up?" Weiss said. "Anyway, they have all joined the police department."

"A nice secure job," the sergeant said. "Who can blame them?"

"This Abe Korn," Weiss said, "he may be a cadaver by now, Sergeant."

"Then at least he won't make trouble," O'Toole said. "Give me a moment, Mr. Weiss, and I'll see if there's anything to be found."

"Take two," Weiss said, cradling the phone between ear and shoulder. He settled back in his chair, put his feet up on the desk, and reached for yesterday's *Forward*.

"Mr. Weiss," the sergeant said in his ear, "your Mr. Korn is in Bellevue."

"What's he doing there?"

"The man tried to commit suicide."

"Did he say why?" Weiss said.

"Not a word."

"Maybe," Weiss said, "he will talk to me."

"I would appreciate any help you could give us," O'Toole said.

"Consider it done," Weiss said.

Forty-eight

It is good to have a policeman in your corner. If he is well placed, he can bring the resources of the department to your aid. If not, he can deceive the opposition into believing that he can.

FROM THE CASEBOOKS OF MORRIS WEISS

Weiss was not overly fond of hospitals. In fact, he hated them. The smell alone turned his stomach. And the memories of those friends who could not be cured or patched up still haunted him. *I will find this Korn, have a short conversation with him, and then leave. There are limits to this Lefkowitz business, and I have come close to reaching mine. I just hope my conversation with Zilberfarb had nothing to do with putting Korn here.*

A uniformed policeman was in front of room 203.
Some job, standing by a hospital door eight hours a day. And I thought I had troubles.

Weiss introduced himself.

"I've been expecting you," the officer said.

Weiss nodded.

"Your man's in there." The officer jerked a thumb at the open door behind him.

"Thank you," Weiss said.

He entered the room.

A short, wrinkled, white-haired man lay motionless in the bed under a white blanket. His eyes were closed. If he heard Weiss enter, he gave no indication of it.

The detective sighed and regarded him silently.

"Mr. Korn," he finally said in Yiddish. "I am a private detective and a friend of your son."

This statement was met with resounding silence.

"Listen," Weiss said. "Losing at Laib Domb's is no reason to take your own life. Believe me, they are crooks there. Everyone knows this. What, my friend, did you expect? The games, they are all fixed."

"You don't say? Tell me something I do not know, mister," he finally said, also in Yiddish.

Weiss nodded.

"Well," he said, "I have been hired to expose them."

"Congratulations. This is very nice. Good luck to you, mister."

Maybe I should just strangle him? Weiss thought.

Abe Korn had still not opened his eyes.

The detective said, "If I do expose them, Mr. Korn, I am sure we can recover part of what you lost, and maybe even the whole thing. It may require a little blackmail, but we will try. But for this you must remain alive, eh?"

Korn finally opened two bloodshot brown eyes and gazed at the detective.

"Thank you, young man," he said still speaking Yiddish, "for your words of encouragement. I appreciate them more than you know. But the truth is, I did not try to kill myself. If I had really tried, I can assure you, I would have, without question, succeeded. You understand me?"

Weiss nodded.

What's not to understand? he thought.

"Please go on, Mr. Korn," he said.

"It was," the patient said, "as they say in English, a hit-and-run."

"They intentionally tried to kill you?"

"There is no question about it. If I had not casually taken a look out of a corner of my eye and seen a car coming at me, I would now be residing in heaven with the angels."

"With the angels, eh?" Weiss said. "A good job if you can get it."

"Frankly, old as I am, I would rather stay here. Let the angels take care of themselves."

"So tell me," Weiss said, "why would they want to kill you, Mr. Korn?"

"Why not? I know their secrets."

And the old man winked.

"What secrets?" Weiss said.

"The big ones."

"Could you give me a hint, maybe?"

"Well, I was, like my father, and his father before him, a carpenter. You know this?"

"Now I do," Weiss said. "And like your son, Yossel?"

"This is true," the old man said. "It runs in the family, you see. So when Laib Domb bought his club some years ago, it was I who was hired to make the changes. You understand me?"

"It does not take an Einstein to understand you, Mr. Korn. But," Weiss said, "can you maybe be a bit more specific?"

"Why not?"

"What changes are you talking about?" Weiss said.

The old man smiled.

"The big ones," he said.

Weiss also smiled pleasantly.

"Mr. Korn, you are still speaking in riddles."

"I will tell you," Korn said.

"That would be very nice of you," Weiss said with a straight face.

"What I mean," Korn said, "are the conditions that let the house win whenever it wants."

The detective raised an eyebrow.

"Such as?" he said.

Korn shrugged a shoulder under his blanket.

"Like the secret back door to make a getaway

easy and the two-way mirrors they have so they can see your hand at the card table. Someone had to build the door and put in the mirrors, young man."

Weiss smiled.

"And that someone was you," he said.

"It was. This was fifteen years ago. Today, I would not do such a thing."

"You have recently threatened to expose them?" Weiss said

"Why would I do that?"

"I am looking for reasons they would want to kill you."

"Who knows?"

"You can not even make a guess?"

"Such people, young man, are capable of anything."

Weiss pulled up the one chair in the room and seated himself.

"Why do you think I am here, Mr. Korn?"

"Because my son, he asked you to drop in on me?"

"I am afraid not," the detective said.

"So," the old man said smiling. "Why *are* you here?"

"Because you were a very big loser at the club last month," Weiss said.

"I was?"

"Mr. Korn, do not play games with me."

"What games?"

"You lost close to a hundred thousand dollars."

"What are you saying? How could a retired carpenter lose that much money?"

"That, my friend, is what I was going to ask *you*."

"*Me*? Better ask them who gave you this so-called information."

Weiss sighed. He was beginning not to enjoy this very much.

"Remember," he said, "your chances are much better with me than with the police. With them you have almost no chance at all."

The old man laughed.

"Police, shmolice," he said. "What do they have to do with this?"

"Plenty, my friend," Weiss said. "What you have been telling me is a bushel of lies."

The old man sat up in bed.

"What lies?" he said. "What are you talking about, mister?"

Weiss again fought back a strong desire to strangle the man. *I would only be ridding the world of a liar* and, *no doubt, a crook*, he thought. *Who would mind except for his son? And maybe not even him.*

"Mr. Korn," Weiss said. "Let us say that you didn't lose a hundred thousand dollars. Let's say instead that you lost only twenty-five thousand, or maybe a mere fifteen thousand. If you want, I can even go down to five thousand, eh? Still, that leaves the major question unanswered."

"What question? Why are you pestering me with this? What is it to you? I am a sick man. They tried to kill me. Isn't that enough for you? You want to finish the job, mister? Go away."

"I will be glad to go away," Weiss said, "if you will answer one question."

"Anything to be rid of you. Go on, ask."

"What were you doing there, Korn?"

"At Laib Domb's?"

"Where else?" Weiss said.

"Gambling. What else is there to do there?"

"Mr. Korn. You have had a hard day," Weiss said. "Are you absolutely sure you want to say that?"

"Why should I not want to say that? I said it, didn't I? Go away, crazy person. I need to rest. I have had more than enough of your madness. Much more than enough!"

And he closed his eyes.

Forty-nine

The life of a private detective is like a very good book. There are all kinds of surprises. The big difference is that there are no reviews to let you know what is coming next.

FROM THE CASEBOOKS OF MORRIS WEISS

"So," Ida said, "*what did you do?*"

"What could I do?" Weiss said. "I went away."

"Just like that?"

"Why not? I am a very obliging fellow."

"Of course you are."

She took his hand.

"And now what will happen?" she said.

The detective shrugged.

"Who knows? At his age and in his condition, he is not going to away. That's for sure."

It was nighttime. The two were in Weiss's flat, in bed together. She in a light-blue nightgown, he in black pajamas. A recording of the Brahms Piano Trio, op.8 as played by Rubinstein and two colleagues, was on the turntable.

"On a better day," Weiss said, "one in which he hadn't almost been run down, Korn would not have made such an obvious mistake. When I pointed this out to him, he turned his back on me and wouldn't say another word."

"So what was this big mistake, Moisheleh?"

"Abe Korn says he likes to gamble," Weiss said. "What kind of gambling is it in a place where you yourself have put in the crooked devices? Something else must be going on. But what? One thought immediately comes to mind. A payoff. Or maybe money laundering. Yossie may be working with his father. And Yossie's friend, Bernie Loft, may have been eavesdropping on this whole crowd. Of course, not all my thoughts are of equal value. This one may be absolutely worthless. But I think that it has some value. Maybe. I am far from sure."

Ida kissed him on the mouth.

"It takes a big man to admit that," she said.

"I am only five foot seven."

"But big in spirit."

"No matter how big, my spirit will not go out on a job alone," he said. "It must be pampered by taking my body along with it."

She kissed him again.

"That," she said, "is for having such a smart spirit."

"Smart, eh?"

"How do you do it, darling?"

The detective thought it over.

"Practice," he said.

"What?"

"Thinking smart thoughts," he said. "Let me give you an example. I know there is a power struggle going on between the factions of Gold's old gang. This, incidentally, includes Gold himself. Take the package I rescued from that locker in Penn Station. Well, this package at one time maybe held a payoff, or blackmail material, or maybe even instructions for pulling some kind of job. But with all the fighting going on, the contents have long ago disappeared."

"So many twists and turns," Ida said.

"True," Morris Weiss said. "And I am the one to untwist them."

Fifty

You know the case is over when there is a solution, or your client has run out of money and can't afford to pay you anymore. When the latter happens I try to continue working for as long as I can in the hope that somehow the money will yet be raised. This is because I am endlessly optimistic and in general a very nice man. At least for a detective.

FROM THE CASEBOOKS OF MORRIS WEISS

Weiss said, "There may be trouble."

"Trouble?" Itchy said. "Who worries about trouble?"

"Trouble only makes it more interesting, you know," Benjy said.

"Actually," Weiss said, "I didn't know that."

"It's true," Itchy said. "Not that baking isn't interesting. It's good, honest work."

"Very honest," Benjy said.

"And it's wonderful," Itchy said.

"If you say so," Benjy said.

"But," Weiss said, "in a different way, eh?"

Benjy sighed.

"Very different," he said.

"After years of being criminals in Warsaw," Itchy said, "we miss the action, that's all."

"That," Weiss said, "is more than enough for my purpose."

The three were seated in a very small but empty restaurant off Orchard Street, drinking coffee out of glasses, the detective's two friends having declined the pastry, which in their own establishment they would have eaten without hesitation.

"So what *is* your purpose?" Itchy said.

"I want you to keep an eye on one Abe Korn."

"And he is where?"

"Resting, at the moment," Weiss said, "in a nice bed in Beth Israel Hospital. They moved him from Bellevue, a testament to his sanity . . . I think."

"As long as it's a nice bed," Benjy said.

"Something is wrong with him?" Itchy said.

"Plenty," Weiss said.

"So out with it," Itchy said. "Let's hear the bad news."

"He was run down in the street and almost killed."

"An accident, of course?" Benjy said.

"We wouldn't be here now if it were an accident," Itchy said, "would we, Morris?"

"Probably not," Weiss said.

"What happened?"

"They tried to kill him," Weiss said.

"But missed, eh?" Itchy said.

"They were not very efficient," Benjy said.

"You must remember," Weiss said, "this kind of work does not attract the best people."

"What did they do to him?" Itchy said.

"Hit him with the end of a fender," Weiss said.

"It was still attached to the car?" Benjy said.

"Unfortunately," Weiss said. "It brushed his leg. But he is not a young man. In his eighties, in fact. Next time they will no doubt do better."

"So," Itchy said, "you think they will try again?"

The detective shrugged.

"They do not take me into their confidence," he said. "But it is a good guess they will."

"And you want us to make sure they miss."

"Yes. And if it is the other way around," Weiss said, "I want you to make sure *he* misses."

"You have gone crazy?" Benjy said.

"I am just trying to keep the old man out of trouble," Weiss said. "He may turn out to be a good witness. Who could do less?"

Itchy shook his head.

"Almost anyone," he said.

"You exaggerate," Weiss said, finishing his coffee.

"What exaggerate? Who exaggerate?" Benjy said.

"He is an old man," Weiss said, "who has just had an unfortunate accident."

"Some accident," Benjy said.

"He may not be thinking clearly," Weiss said. "Who knows?"

"In the meantime," Itchy said, "what will you be doing?"

"Keeping an eye on his son."

"He has a son?" Itchy said.

"His son is, at least, thinking clearly?" Benjy said.

"Not so anyone would notice," Weiss said.

Itchy rose, went to the counter, and brought back another glass of coffee for himself.

"If we stay here much longer," he said, "I might even eat some of their food."

"God forbid," Benjy said.

"What is it all about?" Itchy said.

"Bad things," the detective said. "Very bad things."

Fifty-one

Being the best-dressed man at a party may not help you solve the case, but it will certainly bring you other cases. Prospective clients will think you must be a hotshot private detective to afford such fancy apparel.

FROM THE CASEBOOKS OF MORRIS WEISS

Weiss kept well behind Yossie Korn.

It was bitterly cold. Gloved hands in overcoat pockets, collar pulled up, hat brim pulled down low, the detective was all but invisible. Yossie never looked back.

Weiss had picked him up as he left his building on Third Street off Houston, a little after three in the afternoon, and began trailing after him. *There must be a better way to do this*, he thought. But couldn't figure out what that might be. He started to feel somewhat better when Yossie entered a pawnshop. Through the plate glass window he saw the young man examining a number of handguns and finally selecting one. A small box of bullets came with it. Yossie left the shop carrying his purchase in a brown shopping bag.

Some desperado, Weiss thought.

Again he followed Yossie, but this time it was only back to his flat.

Moscowits and Lupowitz, the Romanian-Jewish restaurant, was just up the block from Yossie's tenement. Weiss hurried to it and entered. Immediately he was enveloped by warmth and fragrant aromas.

The detective sighed.

Being here, he thought, *is just like coming home.* Which, in fact, was almost true. Weiss had spent the early part of the day here, waiting for Yossie to put in an appearance. There were many worse places to wait, but Weiss could think of none better.

He asked for a table at the window. From it, Weiss had a perfect view of Yossie's building.

He ordered flanken with horseradish, dumplings, and sweet-and-sour red cabbage. He asked for a pot of tea, and settled in for the evening.

He fervently hoped that whatever was going to happen happened soon. He didn't want to make a habit of following this man. There were better ways to spend his time. Almost any other way was better than this.

Weiss switched from tea to coffee at nine-thirty in a valiant effort to keep awake. He removed from his overcoat pocket an old copy of the *Forward*, reread a page of Isaac Bashevis Singer's *The Family Moskat*, which had been serialized last year and which the detective had been prudent enough to save just for such an occasion. *Not for nothing am I a detective. I can spot a good story a mile away.*

Yossie Korn again appeared on the street at eleven forty-five. *Bravo*, Weiss thought, *and about time, too.* He was ready. The bill had already been paid. Weiss ran from the restaurant, still climbing into his overcoat, and trying at the same time to get his gloves and muffler out of his coat pockets. The cold air stung him. *When I become rich*, Weiss thought to himself, *I will hire someone to do this for me. It is only fair.*

If Yossie looks back, he is sure to spot me, Weiss thought.

But why should he? And anyway, I am wrapped up like a mummy. It would take an X-ray machine to penetrate all this clothing. Yossie is a carpenter, not a wonder-worker.

It came as no surprise to the detective when he ended up at the gambling club next to the bakery. *Better here*, he thought, *than among strangers.*

He managed a quick smile at his own joke, before following the young man up the staircase.

The club was packed solid.

For a moment, he could not see Yossie. Then he saw him in the center of the large room, slowly making his way toward Zilberfarb's private office.

"Don't do it, Korn," Weiss yelled.

Yossie gave no indication that he had heard.

"Weiss!" a pair of voices called.

Well, someone had heard. The detective looked around. He spotted Blottnick, who waved.

The elder Korn was stepping through the door and had just begun moving through the crowd. Behind him were Benjy and Itchy. They waved.

How nice, Weiss thought. *A convention now.*

"Korn!" he called again. "Don't do it! You will spend the rest of your life in prison!"

Weiss repeated it again. This time, both Korns pulled up short.

Benjy and Itchy saw the salutary effect that these few words had had on their man, and yelled, "Korn! Don't do it!"

No one paid them the least attention. Except the two Korns, who seemed utterly bewildered—as well they might.

Zilberfarb, whom the detective would forever think of as Moisha Pupik, stepped out of his office to see what was going on.

Weiss waved at him, and, at the same instant, caught up with Yossie.

"You will thank me someday," he said to the young man as he hustled him out of the club. "And if you shoot me, I will come back to haunt you."

Behind Weiss, the elder Korn was being carried by Itchy and Benjy, one on either side of him, down the staircase.

"What are you doing?" the elder Korn yelled.

"Stopping a crime wave," Weiss yelled back.

Out of the corner of his eye, to his astonishment, the detective caught sight of Albert Gold in the crowd.

Maybe I have been watching the wrong people, he thought.

"What crime wave?" Korn yelled.

"Yours."

But Weiss was no longer sure this was the crime wave he should be worrying about.

Fifty-two

Yiddish is a wonderful language for a private detective. But by itself, it will not help in solving cases. What it will do, if the private detective is like me, is keep him happy. A happy private detective solves many more cases than an unhappy one. This is a little-known fact. But now that the word is out, everyone will know it.

FROM THE CASEBOOKS OF MORRIS WEISS

"Boris, I have a job for you."

"I am glad to hear it."

"Meet me at the office in half an hour."

"What kind of job is it, if I may ask?"

"An easy one. In the trade, we call it shadowing."

"It sounds very mysterious."

"It's not. It simply means following someone."

"Ah, and you fear the subject might recognize you."

"You should be a detective, Boris."

"I thought I was."

Fifty-three

The last thing a Yiddish private detective wants to do is bring in a Yiddish-speaking criminal. Unless the criminal is very bad. In such cases, it is better to let the police handle matters. Unless, of course, you can persuade the criminal that there are better ways of making money. That will be the day.

FROM THE CASEBOOKS OF MORRIS WEISS

"Dear Mr. Weiss," Fraydela Gold said. "It is so good to see you."

"Thank you. The feeling is mutual."

"Please come in," she said, holding the door open wide.

The detective entered.

What a welcome, he thought. *I must come here more often. If this woman and her son are still out of prison.*

"I'm frozen to the bone," he said.

"Let me make you some tea," his hostess said.

"This would be excellent," Weiss said. "Is Albert home?"

"I think so, yes."

"I would like a word with him," Weiss said.

Mrs. Gold went to the dumbwaiter in the kitchen, opened the small door, and yelled down the shaft.

"Albert!"

"What is it, Ma?"

"Mr. Weiss is here. He wants to speak with you."

"Hold on. I'll be right up."

Mrs. Gold turned and smiled at the detective.

"He is coming right up," she said.

"So I hear," Weiss said.

Presently Albert appeared at the door in an open-neck striped shirt and gray, baggy pants.

"Mr. Weiss," he said.

"Albert," Weiss said, "it is a pleasure to see you."

"It's always nice to see you, Mr. Weiss."

The detective smiled.

"Then at least we agree totally about something," he said.

"More than just one thing, I hope." Albert said.

The detective nodded, walked to the living room window, and peered down. On the corner he saw Boris Minsky. Prying the frozen window open, he waved to him.

"Come up, Boris," he called.

Minsky waved back. Leaving his post, he began walking toward the tenement.

"My associate," he said.

Soon Minsky was among them.

"Boris has been following Albert for the last two days," the detective said.

Albert shrugged.

"He has some pictures for you to see," Weiss said.

"What pictures?" Mrs. Gold said.

"Show them, Boris," Weiss said.

Minsky removed an envelope from his coat pocket and handed it to Albert.

Albert, with his mother peering across his elbow, took out a dozen snapshots from the white envelope and fanned them out in his hand.

"What's this supposed to mean?" Albert said.

"These men you have been meeting are members of your father's old gang. They are currently busy killing each other."

"How would you know?"

"It is my job to know," the detective said. "Or to find informants who do know. You have no doubt been trying to bring them back under one umbrella. Yours maybe, or your father's."

Albert shook his head.

"You can't prove any of this," he said.

"I don't have to. The police are excellent at this sort of thing."

"It wasn't him," Mrs. Gold said.

"Be quiet, Ma," Albert said. "Enough already."

Mrs. Gold ignored her son.

"He was just the messenger boy," she said.

Weiss said, "Whose messenger was he?"

"Watch out what you say, Ma."

"No! I want them to know."

"Ma!" Albert said, slapping his palm against his forehead. "What are you doing?"

"He was *my* messenger," she said. "I wasn't about to stand by and let everything my husband worked for all these years fall apart."

She makes it sound like this gangster was a Wall Street businessman, Weiss thought.

"That's my ma," Albert said, sighing. "Headstrong to a fault."

"I must go now," the detective said. "But I will be seeing you soon."

"When?" Albert asked.

Weiss smiled pleasantly.

"Sooner than you think," he said.

Fifty-four

Lowlifes will not give you a break just because you and they belong to the same ethnic group. In fact, they will attempt to take advantage of you. The thing to do, obviously, is hire an outstanding private detective to get the goods on them. If you live in the right city, you can probably find such a detective in your local phone directory. Hint: look under W.

FROM THE CASEBOOKS OF MORRIS WEISS

Morris Weiss stood under the fire escape, looked up, and shivered. *What a hateful experience this is turning out to be.*

It was two A.M. and bitterly cold. Fortunately, not a soul was in sight.

Only a lunatic would be out on a night like this, Weiss thought. *Or a private detective. At least, it is not snowing. Yet.*

Weiss had on his old army field jacket, which he had dug out of a chest in the hall closet. *I can still smell the mothballs*, he thought. *I will probably smell them all week.*

He had on heavy black gloves, a thick, black woolen scarf, and a peaked cap with earflaps pulled low. Still, his ears felt frozen. And the rest of him wasn't far behind.

Well, he thought, *I have stalled enough. No one is going to come along and do this for me, no matter how long I wait. Although it is always good to hope.*

The detective returned to his car, which was conveniently parked in front of the tenement, removed a small folding stepladder from its trunk, and carted it over to the building. He took one last look around him, saw only darkness, dirty street lamps, and parked cars. Fortunately, there were no policemen. All he needed was to be brought in to Sergeant O'Toole as a miscreant.

Opening the stepladder, he began to climb.

When Weiss reached the lowest rung of the fire escape, he swung over to it and continued his climb to the second floor. There he stopped.

The window he wanted was, of course, frozen to the sill.

I will be, too, if I stay here another moment, he thought.

With considerable effort, Weiss managed to pry the window open. He raised it high and very quietly hoisted himself over the sill and into the room. He heard steam hissing from a radiator. The place smelled musty. He was in a living room. He stood still and waited for his eyes to become accustomed to the darkness. Piles of newspapers littered the floor.

Various articles of clothing hung on the backs of the tired sofa and chairs. Pulp magazines covered the top of a small table near the door. He recognized some of the magazines Albert had mentioned as containing his artwork. Although tempted to stop and examine some, Weiss knew he lacked the time. He could see an old hot plate on the kitchen counter and a sink full of dirty dishes.

Then he moved.

He did not have to search long to locate the two reels of recording tape. They lay on the floor in a closet, just off the living room.

An excellent hiding place, the detective thought. *Only a master criminal would choose it. Or a very dumb one.*

Weiss made his way into the bedroom, which was even mustier than the living room.

He gazed down at the sleeping figure in the bed.

"Wake up, Albert," he said.

"Huh?"

"You have company, lad," Weiss said, in his best imitation of Sergeant O'Toole's brogue.

Albert needed no more prompting. He sat bold upright in bed.

"Who's there?"

"Weiss."

"The detective?"

"Who else?"

"What do you want?"

"To talk to you."

"How did you get in?" Albert said. "This is a hell of a time to pay a visit."

Weiss shrugged.

"It is an excellent time," he said. "How else could I be sure you would be available?"

Albert had on wrinkled white pajamas decorated with large yellow-beaked parrots and green palm trees.

"Nice pajamas," the detective said with a straight face.

"Cut the crap. What do you want?"

"To find out why you did it."

"Did *what*?"

"Set the Laib Domb and Bill Lazio gangs gunning for each other."

"I didn't have to do that," Albert said. "They were already doing it on their own."

"True enough," Weiss said. "But you helped them get going, didn't you?"

"How? Ask the wish fairy?"

"You didn't have to," Weiss said. "Bernie Loft, the WEVD transcription man, was much better than a mere wish fairy. You showed him how he could become rich. You gave him the numbers of Laib Domb and Bill Lazio and their friends. Loft listened in and recorded what he heard."

"I don't even know the man," Albert said.

Weiss pulled up the one chair in the room and seated himself.

"You certainly knew him," he said. "And I'm sure you had no trouble showing him how he could become a very rich man. An idea he would probably never have thought of on his own."

"How did I know him?"

"Through Lefkowitz," Weiss said, "who was friends with your mother and often a guest upstairs. In any case, the telephone conversations between Lazio, Domb, and many of their friends were recorded, and circulated. I would guess they had very few nice things to say about each other, eh? This led to a number of unfortunate killings. Laib Domb would never have shown up alone at Lazio's meatpacking plant if he hadn't been invited by someone he trusted. This was, no doubt, you, Albert. I don't know how Lazio got killed, but I would say the same thing about him. He trusted you, too. After all, you were Gold's son. When the bodies of these two gentlemen were moved around, it was more than an act of disrespect, it was an act of defiance, of all-out war."

"You're crazy. What was in it for me?"

Weiss shrugged.

"Maybe at first only to show your father that you were as capable a criminal as your brother Joey. But then, with all these killings, I suspect you became more ambitious. Maybe you thought you could get rich, or take over part of the organization, or maybe even all of it."

"You can't prove any of this, Weiss, not in a million years."

The detective nodded.

"You are absolutely right," he said. "But that isn't my job, is it? I was hired to find Jake Lefkowitz. I think he will turn up once the word gets out about what was really happening."

Albert slowly got to his feet.

"You're going to tell people?" he said.

Weiss sat back, looked up at Albert, and folded one leg over the other.

Maybe, he thought, *he will try to jump me and I will be forced to beat him to within an inch of his life.*

"I am not going to take out an ad in the *Forverts*," the detective said, "that's for sure."

"What *are* you going to do?"

Now Weiss rose, too.

"Nothing," he said.

"Nothing?" Albert seemed amazed.

"But word has a way of getting around," Weiss said, a smile on his face. "Watch out for your father. They say he has a terrible temper. In fact, Albert, better watch out for everyone."

Then he turned his back on Albert and left the apartment.

But this time he used the front door, not the window.

Fifty-five

Many people confuse vast wealth with great happiness. In the long run this is a very bad mistake. In the short run it isn't so hot either.

FROM THE CASEBOOKS OF MORRIS WEISS

"You ran us a merry chase," Morris Weiss said.

Lefkowitz shrugged.

They were seated at a table in a small Jewish deli a few blocks from the *Forward* building, Weiss with a bowl of vegetable soup and three slices of buttered rye bread, Lefkowitz a cup of coffee and a pastrami sandwich.

Jake Lefkowitz was a medium-sized man in his mid thirties with a full head of curly black hair and a slightly lined face. There was nothing that Weiss would call especially distinctive about him.

Maybe it's the curly hair? Weiss thought. *Who knows? Lefkowitz himself probably doesn't know.*

"When I first met that blond *shiksa*, and saw that she was interested in me, I almost fainted."

212

"Really?"

"Where do I come to such a girl? I am just a poor printer."

"Not so poor," Weiss said.

"What?" Lefkowitz said

"You have a strong union."

And a wife, too. But the detective decided against mentioning that. It was none of his business.

"Anyway," Lefkowitz said, "who could resist?"

I can just imagine the heroic fight he put up.

But Weiss kept this thought to himself, too.

"Listen," the printer said. "We are in bed together when the phone rings. She goes out to the living room to answer it. *What is this?* I think. *Maybe another lover or, God forbid, a husband.* So, very quietly I pick up the phone. I listen to them talking. After a while, I understand. It turns out someone is going to be—what is the word—*rubbed out.* I've heard enough. Next they'll want to rub *me* out. I grab my pants, shirt, and shoes, tiptoe out to the hallway, very quietly open the door, and run for my life. Now I think maybe I can stop running. They say the gangs are finished. Is that true, Mr. Weiss?"

"It is true, Jake. You can come home."

"Thank God," Lefkowitz said. "I wasn't cut out for that kind of life. Not even for blond *shiksas* who get phone calls about killings."

"Who is?" Weiss said.

Fifty-six

When a case is over, it's over. Except sometimes it comes back to haunt you. Do not worry—ghosts can't hurt you; it is people from the old cases that you have to watch out for.

FROM THE CASEBOOKS OF MORRIS WEISS

Ida said, "So explain this."

"Anything," Weiss said.

"What was this Abe Korn doing winning and losing so much money?"

They were in bed together in the detective's flat. He had made up the bed with silk sheets for that special touch. The occasion, he felt, definitely called for it. There were fresh flowers on the bureau and a bottle of wine on the bed table. The afternoon light made Ida's hair, which was spread on the pillow, glow. The apartment was warm and cozy. Weiss stretched, feeling as if he had all the time in the world—at least until the next big case came along. He poured some wine into each of their glasses.

"Having rigged the entire gambling hall," Weiss

said. "He was blackmailing them. The payoffs were his so-called winnings."

Which leaves the Blottnick angle, Weiss thought.

"I've been so busy through all this that I had almost forgotten that this Blottnick had hired me to clean up the gambling club. For a while, things will change there. Blottnick and company, my new clients, have bought a small interest in the gambling hall. If nothing else, they will be guaranteed a winner from time to time. So everyone is happy, except Zilberfarb, who had to make use of Korn's clever getaway door."

Weiss sighed.

"But there is one thing to be thankful for."

"What is that, Moisheleh?"

"At least for us," he said, "it is all over for a while."